'I don't care a d‍ your trust.'

He went on with a k‍ that has a price tag isn't worthy of the name. I need you to love me.'

'I *do* love you,' Dita broke in desperately.

Rider laughed contemptuously. 'You can keep your so-called love. I'll settle for a purely physical relationship to gratify my obsession. Only don't try to dress it up with the name of love.'

Dear Reader

The summer holidays are now behind us—but Mills & Boon still have lots of treats in store for you! Why not indulge yourself in long, romantic evenings by the fire? We're sure you'll find our heroes simply irresistible! And perhaps you'd like to experience the exotic beauty of the Bahamas—or the glamour of Milan? Whatever you fancy, just curl up with this month's selection of enchanting love stories—and let your favourite authors carry you away!

Happy reading!

The Editor

Lee Wilkinson lives with her husband in a three-hundred-year-old stone cottage in a Derbyshire village, which most winters gets cut off by snow. They both enjoy travelling and, recently, joining forces with their daughter and son-in-law, spent a year going round the world 'on a shoestring' while their son looked after Kelly, their much loved German shepherd. Her hobbies are reading and gardening and holding impromptu barbecues for her long-suffering family and friends.

LOST LADY

BY

LEE WILKINSON

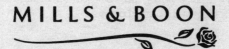

MILLS & BOON LIMITED
ETON HOUSE, 18-24 PARADISE ROAD
RICHMOND, SURREY TW9 1SR

*First published in Great Britain 1993
by Mills & Boon Limited*

© Lee Wilkinson 1993

*Australian copyright 1993
Philippine copyright 1993
This edition 1993*

ISBN 0 263 78283 2

*Set in Times Roman 10 on 11½ pt.
01-9311-53792 C*

Made and printed in Great Britain

CHAPTER ONE

ONLY when Dita was crossing the busy road to the glass and concrete skyscraper that housed Cromford's did she discover she was no longer carrying her small squashy bag.

The winter air was cold and crisp with incipient frost as she hurriedly pushed her way through Manhattan's Friday afternoon crowds back to the bus stop. Seeing the vehicle still standing against the yellow-painted kerb cheered her, but a hasty search by the sympathetic driver proved fruitless.

Clinging to what she guessed might be a forlorn hope, she gave her name and address then told him where she was heading.

When, more than a shade breathless, she finally presented herself at Cromford's reception desk and stated her business, to her relief the lobby clock told her she still had a couple of minutes to spare before her appointment.

'I'm very sorry, Mrs West,' the young, smartly dressed receptionist said with a friendly smile, 'but Mr Stanton has been delayed. If you wouldn't mind going up to the design department and waiting in the foyer? It's on the fifth floor.'

Dita took the lift up and, unbuttoning her stone-coloured mac, settled herself in the small, but luxurious, lounge area.

She didn't mind how long she waited if only Mr Stanton liked her sketches and drawings. When she'd talked to him on the phone, he'd sounded encouraging. It had lifted her spirits like a beacon in the dark.

Getting this job meant everything to her. If she got it she could give the Wilsons some desperately needed help, start to pay off the hospital bills and her rent arrears, and maybe even buy herself a new pair of shoes.

After six weeks of being unemployed *any* job would be more than welcome. But, in this time of recession, vacancies were rare as nuggets of gold. And even more precious.

Starting to feel oddly shivery, though the premises were, if anything, overheated, she glanced at her watch to find she'd been waiting almost an hour. Gritting her teeth, she prepared to sit it out.

Apart from the occasional shrill chirp of a phone and the distant rattle of a printer, everything was quiet. Gradually her lids drooped and her chin sank on to her chest.

Something made her lift her head and open heavy eyes. A tall, wide-shouldered man in a dark, well-cut business suit stood just a foot or two away gazing fixedly at her.

He had a hard, lean face with a hawk-like, Aztec kind of bone-structure. His eyes were grey, his lashes and brows several shades darker than his thick blond hair, which was parted on the left and trying to curl despite a fairly short style.

Convinced she was dreaming, Dita closed her eyes again tightly. When she opened them once more he was still there, still standing watching her with a nerve-racking intenseness.

She scrambled awkwardly to her feet. Her heart seemed to have stopped beating, robbing her brain of blood and her legs of strength. There was a roaring sound in her ears and dizziness assailed her, making her sway.

Resolutely she fought it off and stared at that strong, raw-boned, achingly *familiar* face.

It was well over three years since she'd last seen Rider Barron, and then she'd gone to extreme lengths to make sure she never had to see him again. Now, right out of the blue, here he was.

'I understand you're waiting to see Mr Stanton?' he enquired politely, in his clear, low-pitched voice. A voice that had always sent tingles of excitement up and down her spine.

She nodded, surprised to find that the handsome, dark grey eyes fixed on her were coolly impersonal, showing no awareness at all of who she was, no sign of recognition.

Yet he'd once called her face haunting and unforgettable.

The intervening years had been some of the longest, bleakest of her life, and she felt decades older, but had they changed her *so* much?

Of course in many ways she looked a totally different person. Instead of curling loosely into her neck, her black hair was now long and straight, taken up into a smooth chignon to save hairdressing bills. And in those days she'd weighed almost twenty pounds more, her oval face fuller, her curves more rounded. Even her green eyes had been brighter then, with a brilliant depth of colour that had made them glow like emeralds.

'I'm afraid Stanton won't be back tonight,' he was going on in that cultured accent which held such easy authority. 'But I'll make the time to see you if you'd like to come through to his office.'

What was Rider Barron doing here? Dita wondered frantically, as she picked up her portfolio and accompanied him on legs that felt curiously stiff and alien. Was Cromford's yet another firm gathered into his business empire? If so it was ironic that she'd come here hoping for a job, when a foreclosure by his bank had deprived her of her last one.

His clear grey eyes never leaving her face, he sat down behind Mr Stanton's imposing desk and, with a touch of the careless arrogance she knew so well, waved her to a seat opposite.

Without a doubt he had it all, she thought bitterly— looks, money, background, and an in-built power that set him apart. If he, along with any group of people, had been cast naked and without possessions on a desert island, he would naturally have emerged as their leader.

'Suppose you start by giving me some personal details.' Drawing a pad towards him, he picked up a slim platinum pen, reminding her that he was left-handed.

Self-preservation urged that she tell him nothing, but she *had* to have this job. 'What would you like to know exactly?' Her throat was dry and prickly now, her low, pleasantly husky voice distinctly rough. A spot of colour burnt in each cheek, accentuating her pallor.

'You're Mrs West?'

'That's right.'

For a moment or two he stared at her with aloof concentration, then, sounding as though it was some kind of indictment, commented, 'You're very thin, almost fragile-looking.'

'I can't see that has any bearing on my ability to draw, or do the job efficiently,' she remarked more sharply than she'd intended.

He rubbed an index finger across the hard line of his lower lip. 'It might have if you were frequently ill.'

'I'm very rarely ill,' she stated with truth. 'And I'm a great deal tougher than I look.'

'That's just as well, really.' His grey eyes were penetrating, assessing. Then smoothly he went on, 'How old are you, Mrs West?'

'Twenty-four.'

'It is *Mrs* West?' He sounded as if he had good reason to doubt it.

'Yes, it is,' Dita said stiffly.

After a thoughtful look at the cheap gold weddingring she wore, he asked, 'How long have you been married?'

Resenting what she considered to be an unnecessary question, she answered evasively, 'For some years.'

'A very precise reply.'

Ignoring his sarcasm, she stared at her clasped hands and waited.

'You have no children?'

She shook her head, struggling to suppress the piercing stab of pain his query caused.

Glancing up, she saw that his grey eyes, with their thick, curly fringe of lashes, had deepened to charcoal. Dear God, she thought, panic-stricken, he *knows*.

But the next second he was going on in an even, businesslike tone, 'Where do you live, Mrs West?'

She swallowed hard. 'Greenwich Village.'

'Address?'

'Seven Gooker Street.'

'You're not in employment at the moment?'

'No.'

'Who did you work for previously?'

'Coe's Commercial Art.'

'How did you come to hear of this vacancy?'

'Jonathan Coe suggested I apply.' And it had sounded ideal, the answer to all her prayers. Ranging from commercial designs and illustrations through to fine art work, the job had the variety and challenge she'd always hoped to find. But if she'd had the faintest inkling that Rider Barron would be the one to interview her, eager as she was, wild horses wouldn't have dragged her within a mile of the place.

The irony in his regard made her wonder uneasily if he could read her expression, guess just what she was thinking.

Tapping the end of his pen on the desk, each small sound relentless as a hammer blow, he asked, 'What exactly did you do at Commercial Art, Mrs West?'

The questions seemed to go on and on endlessly. It took a great effort of will to sit up straight and concentrate on answering them lucidly. Inside her head her own voice echoed hollowly, as if she were speaking into a biscuit tin, and she was having some difficulty focusing.

Giving her a brief respite, he reached for the portfolio she'd placed on his desk and began to look through it.

Head bent, trying to subdue the shivers that ran through her, Dita pressed cool fingertips to her throbbing temples and waited.

His voice made her glance up. She found him gazing at her enquiringly, obviously waiting for an answer to a question she hadn't taken in. 'I—I'm sorry...?' she stammered.

He repeated his query, and for the next few minutes fired technical questions at her which showed he had a good working knowledge of art and design.

Finally he closed the portfolio and, pushing it towards her, said with strict formality, 'Thank you, Mrs West. We'll let you know.'

That meant no. All this had been for nothing.

Trying to fight the leaden despair weighing her down, she rose to her feet and, determined he shouldn't see just how shattered she was, managed tonelessly, 'Thank you for your time.'

She had reached the door when he remarked, 'You've forgotten your portfolio.'

Turning, she went back to gather it up, her aching limbs so heavy that she felt as if she were wading through treacle.

He sat quite motionless, watching her.

Glancing at him, she surprised what seemed to be a look of cruel satisfaction on his face. All at once she was convinced that he knew *exactly* how shattered she felt and, whether he'd recognised her or not, was *pleased* about it.

Head high, she started for the door once more.

'How did you get here?' His voice made her pause on the threshold.

'I came by bus.'

The phone rang, cutting through his next question. As he stretched out a hand to lift the receiver, he said peremptorily, 'Wait a minute.'

Ignoring his command, she closed the door behind her and made her escape across the deserted foyer to the lift. Having pressed the call button, she leaned weakly against the wall.

As the lift arrived and she moved to get in, her portfolio came open and a sheaf of her sketches and drawings slid out and cascaded all over the floor.

Crouching, she began to shuffle them together, clumsy in her haste, her urgent desire to get away.

Strong hands closed on her elbows, lifting her, moving her to one side. 'Let me help you.' He was wearing an expensive-looking car coat now, clearly leaving for the night.

'I don't want your help,' she muttered, any attempt at politeness going by the board.

Ignoring her surliness, he collected the loose pages into a neat pile and replaced them, this time fastening the portfolio with care. Instead of passing it to her, however, he tucked it under his arm and, summoning the lift once more, offered, 'I'll take you home,' adding, 'You don't look in a fit condition to be going by bus.'

Refusing to meet his eyes, she said jerkily, 'Thank you, but I'm perfectly all right. I don't need any help.'

'I think you do,' he disagreed. 'You appear to be on the verge of collapse. In fact if I'm any judge it's only will-power that's keeping you on your feet.'

Common sense insisted she could do with some assistance. Her small amount of money had disappeared with her bag, and it was a dauntingly long walk back, even if she'd been feeling well enough.

But to hell with common sense! She'd rather crawl home on her hands and knees than accept help from him. 'Really I can manage. I don't need your help,' she repeated stubbornly.

Disregarding her words, he took her arm and, as the doors slid open, led her into the crowded lift.

When they arrived at the first floor, where the trickle of home-goers was swelling to a stream, he said, 'Wait here a minute,' and went over to the reception desk.

Ignoring his terse instruction, she put on a burst of speed and had almost reached the main doors when, tucking something into his coat pocket, he caught up with her.

Outside it was dark, though the lights of Manhattan made it brighter than day. Frost was sparkling on walls and pavements, settling on the parked cars, and decorating bonnets and trunks with crisp swirls of ice like frilly lace doilies.

As soon as she left the warmth of the building and the cold, misty air wrapped round her, Dita began to shiver uncontrollably.

Sounding angry, he observed, 'Good sense should have told you that mac's far too thin for such weather.'

Good sense *had* told her, but it was the tidiest coat she possessed. 'I'll be plenty warm enough when I get on the bus,' she retorted through chattering teeth. 'There should be one along at any minute.'

Muttering something half under his breath that sounded suspiciously like an oath, he took her arm in a grip of iron and hurried her round the block to a private parking bay.

'I've told you repeatedly that I don't want your help,' she protested, trying to pull free. 'So will you please stop manhandling me?'

'There would be no need to manhandle you if you'd give over behaving like a fool and let me take you home in a civilised manner.'

Still grasping her arm, he unlocked a silver-grey BMW parked slap in front of a notice stating 'Police Vehicles Only'.

Typical, she thought acidly. The whole of the Barron clan, a wealthy family of bankers and politicians who had been a power in New York for generations, tended to ignore the rules and regulations, the petty restrictions that ordinary mortals were subject to.

'Get in,' he ordered, his voice curt.

When she made no move to obey, he pushed her in unceremoniously and slammed the door behind her.

Head pounding, she gave up the unequal struggle and, muttering, 'Bossy swine,' bitterly resigned herself.

Once settled behind the wheel he leaned across to fasten her seatbelt before doing up his own. She caught her breath audibly and froze as the muscular weight of his thigh briefly pressing against her leg made her prey to long-buried emotions.

He gave a little twisted smile, as though unkindly amused by her reaction, before enquiring blandly, 'Where exactly is Gooker Street?'

She told him with the utmost reluctance, not wanting him to know precisely where she lived. Somehow it brought him much too close. Allowed him in a small way back into her life.

He joined the traffic stream silently, his raw-boned profile hard and arrogant.

She recalled another time they'd driven through town together. On that occasion, whereas she'd been quiet and anxious, Rider had been talkative and smiling, looking forward to the party his parents were throwing that evening. But, well aware of her unspoken apprehension, he'd felt for her hand and given it a reassuring squeeze. Then a few seconds later, when they'd stopped at a red light, he'd turned his head and, grey eyes smiling into hers, said softly, 'I love you.'

The words she had never dared hope to hear had filled her with a tumult of joy and happiness...

She cut off the memory with the merciless speed of a guillotine, and reminded herself that even then he'd been deceiving her, having an affair with Julie Dawn behind her back, while he swore *she* was the only woman in his life.

To distract her mind from such disturbing thoughts she forced herself to try and make polite conversation. 'It's a nasty night. I hope you're not going too far out of your way?'

He'd had the penthouse suite at Markman's Hotel on Fifth Avenue overlooking Central Park when she'd known him, so presumably he still had. Unless he'd moved when he married.

When he made no answer, head aching dully, cold inwardly despite the warmth of the car, she heard herself asking inanely, 'Won't your wife wonder where you've got to?'

'I'm not married.' A sudden wry twist to his lips, he added, 'Did you think I would be, Perdita?'

Shock hit her with all the force of a rock fall, momentarily stunning her. So he *had* recognised her. Making a great effort, she said steadily, 'Yes, given the circumstances.'

His sideways glance took in her white face, her clenched hands, the tension in her too thin body. Flatly, he remarked, 'You have a terrible habit of jumping to conclusions.'

'I don't know what you mean,' she denied.

Rider seemed about to say something cutting, then he hesitated, substituting, 'For instance, you've presumed that you won't get the job.'

'Well, I know I won't.' She spoke stonily.

'Oh? And what makes you so sure, may I ask?'

Biting back all the reasons she could have cited, she countered, 'Did you like my sketches?'

'No.' In the moving patterns of light his hawk-like profile looked hard as granite. 'They were competent, even clever, but they lacked sparkle, enthusiasm.'

Her worst fears confirmed, she swallowed what felt like hot shards of glass, and managed, 'I'm sorry you didn't care for my work. I really . . . wanted that job.' She only just stopped herself saying 'needed'.

'I said I didn't like the sketches, but I thought the drawings for *Learning How To Fly* were quite enchanting. They have life and warmth and real charm . . .'

The drawings he referred to were illustrations for a book of fairy-stories she was writing. She hadn't even realised she'd left them in the portfolio.

'My particular favourite was the naughty little boy fairy holding the plump little girl fairy back by her pigtail. Cromford's need someone who can draw with that kind of humour and imagination.'

As she held her breath, he continued, 'Though I make it a policy with any firm I control never to interfere in staffing decisions, I may advise that Mr Stanton take you on.'

'Thank you.' Her voice was a mere thread of sound.

'You've no cause to thank me,' he told her brusquely. 'If I do recommend you it will be because of your undoubted talent.'

It was plain that he harboured no kindly feelings for her. But then she wouldn't have expected him to. He must have felt some measure of discomfort over the way he'd lied to her, and surely that guilt would have caused a backlash, making him hate and resent her?

She took a painful breath. 'How soon did you recognise me?'

'From the first.'

Indignation, humiliation, and hurt mingled. 'Then why on earth did you treat me like a total stranger?'

'I wanted to see how you would handle it.'

That was only part of the reason, she felt sure. There must be a lot more to it than that.

He made no further attempt at conversation and Dita sat mute, trying to sort out her jumbled thoughts and feelings, until they were drawing up in front of the brownstone in Gooker Street.

Rider came round to open her door and, a steadying hand beneath her elbow, helped her out.

Greenwich Village, with Washington Square as its heart, was a diverse neighbourhood which had escaped the rigid grid system. Jazz clubs and trendy boutiques elbowed bookshops and quiet cafés. But both its busy shopping areas and somewhat meandering streets lined with trees and brownstones had a friendly, small-town atmosphere.

On summer evenings tourists thronged the Village, but in this quiet, residential part on a bitter winter night not a soul was in sight; only the street-lamps swathed in diaphanous mist hovered like luminous ghosts.

Together they crossed the road and climbed the broad stone steps. The battered front door groaned its usual protest as he swung it open and followed her inside.

'I live right at the top,' she said quickly, hoping against hope that he'd just turn and go.

Well aware of what was in her mind, he gave her a glinting look. 'I'll see you up.'

Covered by a tattered, threadbare carpet, the first flight of stairs rose steeply from the draughty, ill-lit hall. The other flights had strips of worn brown lino roughly tacked into the treads and were even steeper.

Her forehead clammy with cold perspiration and her limbs strangely uncoordinated, as if her will was no longer in control of her actions, Dita began to climb them. Despite her care she caught her toe and stumbled, and if it hadn't been for Rider's quick reaction she would have fallen.

'These blasted stairs are a death-trap,' he observed curtly. 'Couldn't you find a more convenient apartment on the first floor?'

'I manage quite all right as a rule.' Her pride wouldn't allow her to admit that she couldn't afford anything 'more convenient'.

When they reached the small bare landing at the top of the house, Dita put a hand to her swimming head and muttered, 'Thank you, I'll be fine now.'

'Will you?' he answered grimly. 'Where's your key?'

For a moment she stared at him uncomprehendingly, then she bit her lip hard, struggling against despair. She'd only ever had one key to the door, and that had been in the bag she'd lost.

'Or perhaps you don't require a key?' Rider went on blandly. 'Maybe your husband's at home?'

The mockery in his voice gave her the stimulus she needed. Thinking, May God forgive me, she squared her shoulders and lied hardily, 'Well, if he isn't, I'm sure he soon will be. Goodnight, and thank you again.'

Her words had been intended as a positive dismissal, and Rider's wolfish grin told her he recognised them as such. But he merely stood there waiting, tall and distinctly dangerous.

If only he'd *go*, she thought helplessly. All she wanted to do was close her eyes and sink into oblivion, even if it was on the icy landing.

With deadly softness, he asked, 'Aren't you going to knock and see?'

Somehow he *knew* she was lying and he had no intention of letting her get away with it.

'There's no one there,' she admitted stonily. 'And I haven't got a key. I lost my purse.'

He put his hand in his coat pocket and produced her missing bag.

'W-where did you get that?' she stammered.

'Someone from the bus terminal phoned to say it had been found. Before I came up to the design department I gave instructions that one of Cromford's staff should collect and sign for it and leave it at Reception.'

Dita stared at him, recalling dazedly how when he'd caught up with her in the lobby he'd been slipping something into his pocket.

'Why didn't you give it to me straight away?' she demanded.

'Do you really need to be told?'

Of course she didn't. Not having her bag put her at a disadvantage, made her that much more dependent on him.

'So is there any further need to stand out here in the cold?' he prodded.

Only too aware that it would be no warmer inside, she fumbled for the key with clumsy fingers and unlocked the door.

She could almost wish the bag hadn't been found, she thought wearily. Rider was the very last person she wanted here, seeing the way she lived. But she was unable to prevent him following closely on her heels.

Having pressed the light-switch, she turned to carry the war into home territory. 'So you knew who I was before you even saw me?'

'Yes, I knew.'

As they spoke, their breath vapourised on the air and Rider muttered an imprecation.

'How did you know?' she demanded, anger and bitterness churning inside her as she faced the fact that he'd been playing with her from the start.

'A couple of months ago when I was at Coe's on business I caught a glimpse of you. At first I could hardly believe it *was* you I'd seen, and when I checked the staff records the name was wrong.

'I paid another visit. The second time I got a better look and knew it was you, no matter what you were calling yourself. Jonathan Coe spoke very highly of you, so I mentioned there would be a vacancy at Cromford's and suggested you might apply for it.'

'Why?'

'Why do you think, Perdita?'

In no mood for guessing games, she said shortly, 'I haven't the faintest idea, unless you wanted to crow over me.'

His voice dangerously quiet, he asked, 'Now why would I want to do that?'

'Because you're an unprincipled swine?' she suggested sweetly.

He let that ride, and, his fair, well-marked brows drawing together, remarked, 'It's like the Arctic in here.'

'The central heating doesn't work.' As his frown intensified, she said hastily, 'But the electric fire does.'

She forbore to mention that she had no quarters to feed the rapacious meter, and even when she had what little heat she could coax from the old, single-bar fire just disappeared into the rafters.

Judging by Rider's expression, however, he'd instantly made his own assessment, and was far from impressed.

Sinking into a chair, she watched with impotent anger as he began to prowl about, opening doors to peer into the dark, cramped kitchen and the dingy bathroom.

The main room was large, and once she'd put down some cheap, bright rugs to hide the old, cracked floor-covering, and painted the grubby walls in pastel colours, it had, despite the shabby furniture, started to look more homely.

Apparently he didn't think so. 'How the hell do you live in a dump like this?' he asked disgustedly.

Seeing the place through his eyes, how bleak and cheerless it looked in the harsh light from the overhead lamp, she found herself unable to defend it. Her lips tightening, she made no answer.

'How long have you been here?'

'Since I started working for Coe's.'

'And how long is that?'

'About eighteen months.'

Strolling over to the narrow divan, which was pushed against a wall and strewn with cushions to turn it into a couch for daytime use, he stood looking down at it. 'Is this where you sleep?'

'Where else?' She tried to sound flippant.

The grey eyes glittered. 'And what about your husband?'

'What about him?' Fear of betraying too much and leaving herself unprotected made her sound positively belligerent.

'There's no point in trying to keep up the pretence,' he informed her flatly. 'It's quite obvious you live here alone. So where is your husband? Why isn't he with you?'

'That's none of your business,' she objected.

With a sigh, Rider began, 'I really think——'

'Think what you like,' she broke in, at the end of her tether. 'I don't feel well enough to argue.'

'I can believe it. You look as if you're running a temperature.'

'I'm coming down with a cold, that's all,' she insisted.

Reaching out, he put one cool hand on her burning forehead while the other encircled her wrist. She flinched and tried to pull away. 'Keep still,' he instructed shortly, then stood towering over her, lean fingers resting lightly on her pulse. 'You may need a doctor.'

She couldn't afford a doctor. 'The only thing I need is to lie down,' she said, her voice ragged. 'If you'd just go and leave me alone I could get to bed and sleep it off.'

'I haven't the slightest intention of letting you stay in this ice-box without anyone to take care of you. You'll end up with pneumonia, and I don't want your death on my conscience.' He released her wrist. 'So collect whatever clothes and things you need and let's get out of here.'

Afraid she was losing her grip on sanity, she protested hoarsely, 'But this is my home. I've nowhere else to go.'

With a soft determination, he said, 'You're coming with me, and there's an end to it.'

'Don't you believe it!' Then carefully, so she wouldn't betray too much emotion, she asked, 'Why all this concern?'

'Let's say that I feel some responsibility for you.'

'I don't see why you should.'

'We were close friends once,' he said, his tone flat, devoid of expression.

'That was a long time ago and things have changed.' Then, with more than a hint of desperation, 'Oh, *why* didn't you give me my purse and let me make my own way home?'

Coolly, he admitted, 'I was curious to see where you lived... And it's just as well I was. Now I know what the conditions are like I've no intention of leaving you here, so get your things.'

Grey eyes on her face, he waited a moment. When she made no move to obey, he repeated inexorably, 'I'm taking you to my place, so pack what you need and let's get going.'

Dita shook her head, mutely defying him. She felt like death. All she wanted was to be by herself, to crawl into bed and seek the oblivion of sleep. The mere thought of having to go to Rider's penthouse was anathema to her. She couldn't bear to see the place again, to have the memories she'd fought so hard to free herself from overwhelm her once more.

His patience plainly exhausted, he announced, 'This is your last chance.'

Her soft mouth set, she shook her head with even greater determination. 'I don't want to go anywhere with you.'

He left her sitting there feeling oddly detached and swimmy while he gathered up her toilet things, some nightwear, and a change of clothing, all of which he thrust into a brown paper carrier bag.

'Now, then,' he said, looming over her, 'are you coming willingly or do I have to use force?'

CHAPTER TWO

DITA tried to read his expression, to judge just how serious he was, but his face seemed oddly blurred.

Sounding a lot braver than she felt, she stated, 'I've absolutely no intention of going anywhere, and you can't make me.'

'Do you want to bet? If I have to, I'll throw you over my shoulder and carry you.'

He *was* quite capable of putting his threat into operation, she admitted. Past experience had taught her that when he really wanted something he let nothing stand in his way.

And he wanted *her*, despite his association with Julie Dawn...

A steely grip beneath her arm, he urged her to her feet. Wanting to fight but unable to find the strength, she gave in and allowed him to escort her down the stairs to the waiting BMW.

Because she was leaning back in her seat, eyes closed, listening to the swish of the wipers as they cleared freezing mist from the windscreen, it was some time before she realised they were driving out of town. Alarmed, her lids flew open and, sitting up with a jerk, she peered out of the window, demanding sharply, 'Where are you taking me?'

'Home,' he said succinctly.

'But I thought...'

'Since we last met I've bought a house in the Catskills. These days I only use the penthouse during the week.'

24

She hadn't relished the idea of going to his apartment, but neither did she want to be taken upstate into the wilds.

His wry sideways glance told her he knew exactly how she felt. It also told her he was expecting some strenuous opposition. But, starting to feel too rotten to care overmuch, she made none. It would be no use, she thought defeatedly. Though she had often fought Rider in the past, she'd never managed to win.

As they left the last built-up area behind them and headed for the southern rim of the mountains, Dita gradually relaxed the tight hold she was keeping on herself and slipped into an uneasy doze.

They were passing through a quiet rustic village when she next opened her eyes. 'Where are we?' she asked thickly.

'Owlport,' he answered, and, as they left the lighted windows of the white clapboard houses behind them and began to climb a serpentine road, added, 'We're practically home.'

Stiff and aching, longing to lie down in a proper bed, all Dita could feel was a vast relief.

He was as good as his word. In a moment or two, leaving the mist-shrouded trees behind them, they followed a curving drive to a level platform of open ground and drew to a halt in front of an old house.

It had been built in the style of an English manor house, with mullioned windows, low gables at odd angles, and a conglomeration of crooked chimneys. A lantern gleamed above the doorway, and shafts of yellow light shone through its diamond-leaded panes, turning the mist pressing the glass to gold.

Rider steadied her as she stumbled out of the car and, an arm around her waist, propelled her through the heavy front door and across a wood-panelled hall. In the comfortable sitting-room he helped her off with her mac and steered her to a low couch in front of a blazing log fire.

'As soon as you've had a bowl of soup or something...' he began.

She shook her head. Her throat felt raw and her appetite was non-existent. 'I don't want anything to eat.' Seeing he was about to overrule her, she went on hoarsely, 'But I would like a drink, and perhaps an aspirin.'

'You look as if you need more than an aspirin,' he disagreed grimly.

'I'm sure it's just a cold,' she said with less than truth, then, as if determined to convince herself as well as him, 'I'm not really ill.'

Studying her extreme pallor, the smudges of fatigue beneath the almond eyes, the hectic flush lying along her high cheekbones, he said, 'I wouldn't like to bet on that.'

'I'll be right as rain by morning,' she insisted.

His silence more telling than any argument, he walked away and vanished through a door at the far end of the room.

She *couldn't* be ill, Dita thought frantically. With so many debts and the Wilsons relying on her for help, she needed to start work as soon as possible...

'Try this.' Rider stooped and folded her hands around a porcelain mug. 'It'll help your throat.'

Gratefully she sipped the warm honey and milk drink which was liberally laced with brandy. Sitting down opposite, he waited until the mug was empty, then took it from her and said, 'I've asked Mrs Merriton to make up a bed for you. Why don't you stretch out on the couch until it's ready?'

She hesitated, *wanting* to lie down but unwilling to remove her shoes, ashamed that he should see the insides lined with thin cardboard to cover where the soles were almost worn into holes.

He squatted and, giving her no chance to protest, slipped them off. Turning the court shoes over in his big hands, he examined them, before dropping them by the hearth with a wry grimace.

Humiliated, not by her poverty, but by his reaction to it, she flushed scarlet. His jaw tightened, and he seemed about to say something. Then, obviously deciding against it, he positioned a cushion beneath her dark head and swung her legs on to the couch, before switching off the main lights.

As the latch clicked behind him, she relaxed. It was warm and comfortable and quiet, the only sounds the soothing tick-tock of the grandfather clock and a soft rustle as the burning logs settled in their cradle.

Within seconds her heavy lids closed and oblivion came like a comforting blanket tucked around her by loving hands.

Dita surfaced slowly and with difficulty and lay in a kind of stupor while small details filtered into her consciousness. She felt relatively normal now, except for a raging thirst and eyelids that seemed to be glued shut.

Yet she had odd, disjointed memories of tossing and turning, aching in every limb and burning with a furnace heat. She recalled something blessedly cool sponging her hot face and body, hands lifting and supporting her while she sipped various potions...

Perhaps it had just been a nightmare, caused by the fear of being ill?

When she managed to prise open her eyes, everything was blurred and wavy, as though she were in a strange underwater world of moving light and shade. With an incoherent murmur, she struggled to sit up.

A man rose from a chair by the bed and pressed her gently back against the heaped pillows. 'Take it easy, now,' he said.

After a moment his lean, strong-boned face swam into focus. *Rider*... What was *Rider* doing in her apartment?

Only it *wasn't* her apartment. She looked around dazedly. It was a strange room, with a pale, floral-patterned carpet and handsome furniture. Bowls of spring flowers were scattered about and a bedside lamp glowed softly. Through the casement windows she could see grey morning light filling the sky and snowflakes drifting down.

She tried to speak, but all that emerged was a hoarse croak.

'Thirsty?' he asked, bending over her.

She nodded.

Sliding an arm behind her bony shoulders, he held a small glass of cool orange juice to her parched lips. She drank greedily, and when he would have taken the glass away reached out and put her own hands round it.

He refilled it from a jug on the cabinet, and, when it was empty once more, took it from her and plumped up the pillows to support her back.

'Feeling better?' he asked, sitting on the edge of the bed and studying her.

'Yes, thank you,' she mumbled, her brain swaddled in layers of cotton wool.

'That's good. We were starting to get really concerned about you.'

After an abortive attempt to free her mind from the enveloping mass and *think*, Dita asked the classic question, 'Where am I?'

'At Rider's Keep.'

'Rider's Keep?' she echoed.

'It's a house that my great-grandfather had built when he emigrated from England. His name was Rider.'

'What am I doing here?'

'Your apartment was like an ice-box and you were ill, so I brought you home with me, remember?'

'Yes, I think so,' she said uncertainly.

'It's just as well I did,' he went on. 'You've had a nasty bout of flu.'

Dita pressed waxy fingers to her temples. 'How long have I been here?'

'Four days.'

For a moment or two she struggled to take it in, then, 'Four days!' she cried in horror. The very last thing she wanted was to be beholden to Rider Barron.

Reading her thoughts with deadly accuracy he said, 'And you'd almost rather be dead than owe any thanks to me?'

'You're one word wrong,' she retorted.

'Well, I much prefer you alive. You see, I have plans for you, Perdita.'

Though he spoke lightly, as though it was meant as a joke, her blood ran cold. 'Plans?' she repeated. 'What do you mean, plans?'

'You'll have to wait and see. Anticipation hones the pleasure, or so I've been told.'

He brushed a strand of dark hair away from her cheek and tucked it behind her ear, smiling wolfishly when she flinched away. Then, rising to his feet, he asked, 'Would you like a cup of tea?'

She nodded, and watched him depart with relief. His manner had been so avuncular when he'd asked about the tea that she wondered if she was mistaken in believing he'd previously been trying to frighten her.

A door to the left stood a little ajar, showing a flash of primrose tiles. Pushing back the bedclothes, she lowered her feet to the floor and, feeling ridiculously weak, made her shaky way to the bathroom.

She washed her hands and face and, finding her own toilet bag on the shelf, cleaned her teeth and pulled a comb through her hair. It was as much as she could do to lift her arm, and her scalp felt tender. Trembling with the exertion, she returned to bed.

She was barely settled when the door opened and Rider came back carrying a steaming cup.

A frown drew his well-marked brows together. 'I see you've been up. You shouldn't have chanced it alone. You've had nothing to eat for days; you must be as weak as the proverbial kitten.'

Sipping the sweet, milky tea, she asked uncomfortably, 'Who's been looking after me?'

'Mrs Merriton, mostly. Luckily she was a nurse before she became my housekeeper.'

'Oh... I hope I haven't caused her a lot of extra work.'

'Don't worry, she offered. She seems to have taken you under her wing. At one stage she even referred to you as a "poor lamb".'

He grinned, his teeth very white, his eyes sardonic beneath level brows. 'You may not realise it, but that's akin to Boudicca turning into Florence Nightingale.' He took the empty cup, adding, 'She'll be here shortly with some breakfast for you. I'll shower and change while you try to eat it.'

For the first time Dita registered the fact that his blond hair was rumpled and golden stubble roughened his jaw. He was already dressed, but tieless, his shirt unbuttoned at the neck, his trousers a little creased, as if he'd slept in his clothes.

She was startled. Surely he hadn't been sitting up with her?

The door had scarcely closed behind him when it opened again to admit the housekeeper carrying a tray.

Mrs Merriton was an elderly, sour-faced woman with short iron-grey hair and rather large teeth which she showed now in a rare smile of satisfaction. 'Well, that's better. It's nice to see you wide awake and taking notice.'

'I'm sorry if I've been a lot of trouble,' Dita apologised.

Settling the daintily laid tray across her knees, the housekeeper said, 'It's been no trouble at all. Mr Rider was going to hire extra help, but I wouldn't hear of it.' She removed the cover from a small silver dish of scrambled eggs, and poured a glass of creamy milk. 'There now, see what you can manage of that. It'll be a weight off his mind when you start eating. He's been very worried about you.'

I bet! Dita thought derisively. Yet perhaps, conscience suggested, she wasn't being fair. Even if he disliked her, he'd been concerned enough to refuse to leave her alone in an unheated apartment. And now it appeared he'd been sitting up with her.

Although the top of her mouth hurt and she had no appetite, Dita made an effort and ate a small piece of bread and butter and a spoonful of the fluffy egg, but she was asleep almost before she'd finished the milk.

Next time she stirred and opened her eyes it was nighttime, and the room was dark except for a single lamp casting a diffused light. She felt curiously alert and clearheaded, very different from her first muddled awakening.

Rider was sprawled in a chair close by, his heavy lashes fanning on to high, broad cheekbones, his firm mouth relaxed in sleep. All at once her heart turned over, as it always had in the past. She'd loved him so very much.

Not at first, though. At first, in spite of her attraction, she'd been far too wary. Knowing that all he wanted was an affair, she'd been resolved to keep him at bay until he grew tired of his pursuit.

But she hadn't been prepared for his persistence, his unswerving determination. Nor, after a childhood of giving and receiving quiet, restrained affection, had she been prepared for her own fierce feelings.

She sighed deeply, and in the dimness suddenly became aware that Rider was awake and watching her, his grey eyes gleaming between half-closed lids.

'Are you thirsty?' he asked.

'No, I just can't sleep.'

Instantly she regretted her admission when he said with unconcealed satisfaction, 'Then try sitting up for a while and we'll talk.'

'Talk?' she echoed with dismay, as he helped her up. 'What is there to talk about?'

He lifted the pillows behind her and, one arm each side of her slim body, imprisoning her, said with silky menace, 'As it's over three years since we've seen each other, three years since you ran out on me, we should have plenty to talk about, wouldn't you say?'

Consternation turning to fear, she shook her head mutely.

'Then I'm afraid we disagree. For instance there are a number of questions I'd like answers to.'

Well aware that for the word 'like' she could substitute 'intend to have', she inwardly quailed.

'Suppose you start by telling me your husband's name?'

Choosing her words with care, and keeping her voice as level as possible, she said, 'His name's Stephen . . . Stephen West.'

'What does he look like?'

'He has blue eyes and red hair. His friends used to call him Ginger . . .' She stopped speaking abruptly.

Not seeming to notice her slip, Rider went on, 'How long had you known West when you married him?'

Avoiding Rider's eyes and trying to ignore the way his closeness made her heartbeat quicken and the breath catch in her throat, she prevaricated. 'Not very long.'

'When did you meet him?'

She didn't want to answer Rider's questions, but if she refused point-blank he was bound to wonder why. Feeling trapped, threatened, she admitted, 'When I moved to New York.'

'The same time you met me.' It was a statement rather than a question. The question followed, quiet but lethal. 'And you deliberately kept his existence a secret?'

'I didn't do anything of the kind.'

'So why did you never mention him?'

Rattled, she flared, 'I don't know. But it certainly wasn't deliberate.' And it hadn't been. She'd never mentioned Stephen simply because at that time he'd had no significance whatsoever in her life.

'Did you see him while you were going out with me?'

Shocked at the direction Rider's suspicions were taking, she said, 'He had the apartment above mine so I could hardly fail to see him occasionally. But I didn't meet him behind your back, if that's what you mean. *You* were the one who cheated...'

Rider's face contorted momentarily as though he was in pain. 'I didn't cheat on you, Perdita. From the first minute I saw you sitting behind that damned desk I never so much as looked at another woman.'

For just a few moments the convictions of the past three years were badly shaken by the ring of truth in his voice. Then she steadied herself. What kind of fool did he take her for? She *knew* that was a lie.

She stared at him, mutely repudiating his words.

His grey eyes hardened to polished granite, and her heartbeat marked the seconds that passed before he resumed his interrogation. 'So it must have been a whirlwind courtship? Off with the old love, on with the new?' Then, like a cobra striking, 'You *did* love him?'

Though she knew instinctively that it wasn't the answer Rider wanted, Dita refused to deny it. 'Yes, I loved him. But it wasn't like that...'

'What was it like? Did he manage to seduce you...?' Then, instantly, 'No, I can hardly believe that.'

'Why not?' she demanded bitterly. 'You managed it easily enough.'

He smiled sardonically. 'I wouldn't say that. It took a lot of time and patience... No, I'd never call you *easy*, Perdita.'

When she failed to react to his taunt, he suggested, 'Unless of course you're making the whole thing up?'

Thrown by his sudden change of tack, she stammered, 'M-making the whole thing up...? I don't know what you mean.'

'I mean I doubt the existence of this invisible husband of yours. I think you're just calling yourself Mrs West.'

In a strangled voice, she objected, 'Why on earth would I do that?'

He was much too near, his hard face only inches away from hers. 'My guess is, in order to help you disappear so successfully.'

'Then your guess is wrong.' She refused to elaborate.

His mouth thinned. 'If you *are* married, why are you living alone?'

'I've told you, it's none of your business.'

'Are you divorced or separated?'

'No.'

'Then why isn't he taking care of you? And don't try to tell me he is. I've seen where you live, seen the state of your shoes. He must be an absolute louse to leave you to struggle on alone when you're out of work.'

Guilt tearing at her, she cried wildly, 'Stephen isn't to blame for anything. None of it's his fault.'

'If you want me to believe that you'll have to tell me why he isn't helping to support you.'

Pushed beyond endurance, she cried, 'Because he's dead! Now are you satisfied?'

She heard the hiss of Rider's breath, watched his face tighten and lose colour. 'I'm sorry,' he apologised quietly. 'You should have told me.'

'Why should I have told you?' she demanded. 'It has absolutely nothing to do with you.'

'Now there I must disagree.' His tone seemed to hold a silky menace. Then, grey eyes shuttered, hiding his thoughts and intentions, he asked, 'How long have you been a widow?'

'A few weeks,' she answered baldly.

A muscle jerked betrayingly in Rider's jaw. 'What caused his death?'

She hesitated, then said, 'He was badly hurt in a crash on the interstate.'

Rider homed in on that immediately. 'You mean he wasn't killed outright?'

'No.' Dita bit her lip. 'He suffered extensive injuries as well as brain damage.'

'When did the accident happen?'

'Just before Christmas.' Purposely she failed to add that it had been three years previously.

'Was he conscious?'

She brushed the back of her hand across her eyes. 'No, he was in a coma.'

'It must have been hell to see him like that.' Rider sounded shaken.

Her voice barely above a whisper, she said, 'His doctor told me there was virtually no hope, but I couldn't believe it. I used to go and sit with him for two or three hours every day.'

Every day for nearly three long years. And, on each visit, guilt had sat with her like an old friend.

Despite her normally heavy workload she'd always made time to go to the hospital, sometimes during the day, sometimes in the evening. Unwilling, *unable*, to accept the doctor's verdict, she'd talked to Stephen, held his hand, played his favourite tapes, taken him scented flowers . . .

'Dear God,' Rider muttered.

She waited, only too aware that his quick brain would soon make the connection between what she'd just told him and her poverty.

Sure enough, after a moment he asked the question she'd known was inevitable. 'Did he have personal insurance cover?'

'No.' And neither had the Wilsons.

'Any compensation?'

She shook her head.

'So who took care of his medical expenses?'

'I did.'

Rider said something short and savage under his breath before asking roughly, 'How the hell did you cope?'

She paused, unwilling to admit what a struggle it had been. Even when she'd been in full-time employment and writing short stories, she'd needed to take any additional work she could get, sometimes sitting up half the night illustrating greetings cards or labouring over private commissions.

When that sort of work was in short supply she'd looked for evening jobs, waiting on tables, washing dishes, pumping petrol, anything that would help to pay the bills.

But she could hardly tell Rider that.

Lifting her chin, she assured him, 'Most of the time I managed quite well.'

It was obvious he wasn't fooled for a minute. 'It's a pity you hadn't a family to help. Your father died, didn't he?'

'Yes, he had a heart attack. It was after that that I moved to New York.'

'Have you no other relatives?'

'Not close ones. The few I do have live in England. My mother died when I was a baby, and my father moved to Washington, DC after he was given a post at the British Embassy...'

She'd kept talking, *babbling*, to stave off further questions; now she added quickly, 'If you don't mind I'd like to lie down again. I'm feeling tired.'

He nodded and got to his feet. 'Try to get some more sleep.'

When she was settled he stood looking down at her. His face was set and oddly angry. As though talking to himself, he remarked, 'No wonder you look like a ghost. But from now on things are going to be very different.'

From now on things are going to be very different.

He'd said those self-same words to her once before and it had marked a turning-point in their relationship. That was the night he'd kissed her for the very first time, provoking a passionate response she'd been powerless to hide...

Unconsciously she sighed and moved restlessly in the big bed, the memory of his mouth claiming hers disturbing her almost beyond endurance.

'Still awake?' Rider asked, with what sounded like genuine concern. 'Shall I get you a warm drink?' Without waiting for an answer he went out, leaving the door slightly ajar.

A rectangle of light spilled from the passage, illuminating a strip of creamy, rose-patterned carpet. Falling snow whispered against the leaded panes. The clock showed almost two-thirty.

She had pushed herself into a sitting position and was propped against the pillows when he returned a few minutes later with a comforting mug of hot chocolate.

As soon as she'd finished it, he put the mug on the bedside table and bent over her to settle her down again. Curiously, she asked, 'Rider...why have you been sitting up with me?'

Silently he studied her skin, which looked semitransparent, the hollow cheeks, the green eyes that appeared too big for her face. 'Someone had to. It seemed to make more sense for Mrs Merriton to look after you during the day while I was working, then for me to take over at night.'

He'd answered her question, yet not answered it. 'But you must have been losing your sleep,' she objected uneasily. 'Surely a nurse would have been...' She hesitated.

He quirked a brow. 'An easier option?'

'Well, yes.'

'Possibly. But I wanted to watch over you.' His smile was crooked, belying the implied tenderness in his words.

'Why?' Her voice emerged as a mere breath of sound.

'For several reasons. You see, I've often thought about what I might do if I ever met you again. I've wondered how I could get you in my power, imagined how much I'd enjoy having you helpless in my hands.'

He laughed harshly at the look on her face. 'Does that sound melodramatic? I suppose it does. But you did ask.'

She wished she hadn't. Though surely he was just joking?

Fighting down the panicky fear that constricted her lungs and made her heart beat erratically, she said steadily, 'I'm sure it would be better for you to get a good night's sleep rather than sit there gloating... If that's really what you've been doing.'

'Oh, it is indeed.'

The assurance shook her, as it had been meant to. Jerkily, she asked, 'Do you really hate me *so* much?'

'What makes you doubt it?'

'*Why* do you hate me?' Passion and bewilderment mingled. 'It wasn't my fault.'

'You ran out on me.'

Furiously, she cried, 'And of course a mere secretary couldn't be allowed to run out on the great Rider Barron, no matter what he'd done.'

He brushed an angry hand over his thick blond hair. 'Have you any idea how I felt when I got back and found you'd gone?'

'Have you any idea how *I* felt when I found you were the father of Julie Dawn's child?'

His voice full of bitterness, he muttered, 'In those days I was fool enough to think you trusted me.'

'I *did* trust you.'

'Like hell! If you'd trusted me you'd have waited to hear my explanation.'

'Explanation!' she choked. 'What explanation could there possibly have been? You'd *admitted* everything.'

'And you believed it,' he said wearily.

'Certainly I believed it. Why on earth would you have made a public declaration if it hadn't been the truth?'

'I'll leave you to work that one out. In the meantime...'

'You're enjoying having me helpless in your hands!' Her face full of scorn, she mocked his earlier words.

He gave a cruel little smile. 'Immensely.'

'But why?' she demanded, trying to hide the stab of apprehension. 'What do you hope to gain?'

'I'm keeping that for a surprise.'

A shudder ran through her. Gritting her teeth, she told herself she wouldn't allow him to scare her. As soon as she felt a bit stronger she could walk out of here and he couldn't stop her. But all the same she felt afraid. Caught in a trap.

When he resumed his chair, she closed her eyes and turned her back on him. But she could *feel* him watching her.

It was a long time before she slept.

CHAPTER THREE

DITA stirred and sighed, part of her mind recognising the fact that she was dreaming. But she didn't want to wake up and face reality. It was such a lovely dream ...

She was in Central Park lying on sun-warmed grass, golden leaves making a dazzling mobile above her head, but all her attention was focused on the man stretched with graceful ease by her side.

Propping himself up on one elbow, Rider leaned over to kiss her. She closed her eyes with a sigh of pleasure as his lips began to move lightly, seductively against her own.

When he would have lifted his head, her eyes still closed, she ran her hands into his thick fair hair and, with a little incoherent murmur, drew his mouth back to hers.

He kissed her again, with sweet abandon, then murmured, 'If I'd known you were going to be so receptive, I might not have slept in the chair last night.'

Her long black lashes lifted and, confused, she stared up into the strong face so very close to hers. It was the same man who had been kissing her, but, instead of Central Park in the autumn, she was lying in bed in the snowy light of a winter morning, and he was sitting by her side.

As her mind cleared and his mocking words penetrated, she felt her face grow hot. Bracing her arms, she pushed herself upright. 'I was dreaming,' she said defensively. 'Dreaming Stephen was kissing me.'

Rider's jaw clenched, and as a kind of dark, primitive fury flared briefly in his grey eyes she realised she'd instinctively chosen the right weapon to pierce his armour of satisfaction.

After a second or two, her voice husky, she asked, 'Why did you wake me?'

His face wiped clear of expression, he answered, 'I wanted to talk to you before I left for town.'

Seeing the white flakes still swirling past the windows, she demurred, 'Will you be able to drive into town with all this snow?'

'The freeway will be clear.' He sounded casual, unconcerned.

Trying to hide her unbidden anxiety, she objected, 'But you have to get to it.'

'When I bought the Keep a couple of years ago I also bought a four-wheel-drive Range Rover, with this kind of weather in mind.'

Her fear for his safety got the better of caution, and she blurted out, '*Must* you go? Can't you keep in touch by phone?'

'I could if it were just ordinary business. In fact that's what I have been doing for the past few days. But this is a matter I want to handle personally.' An ironic gleam in his eyes, he observed, 'If you go on like this you'll almost have me believing you'd care if anything happened to me.'

Dita bit her lip and said nothing.

'Apart from nightwear,' he went on, after a brief pause, 'is there anything else you'd like bringing from your apartment?'

She shook her head. 'I'll be going home soon.'

'Don't be a fool,' Rider rebuked her shortly.

'I should be up by the weekend,' she insisted, her face stubborn, her urgent desire to get away unabated.

'If by "up" you mean an hour or so out of bed, I agree. But there's no way you'll be able to fend for yourself in an icy cold apartment. You don't seem to realise how ill you've been. It will probably be another week before you're fit to do anything much apart from convalesce.'

'I can't stay here all that time.' Thinking of her mounting debts, the huge pile of hospital bills, the promise she'd made to Paul Wilson's mother, made her voice rise hysterically. 'I've commitments. I must start work as soon as possible.'

'You won't be able to work if you make yourself ill again,' he pointed out. 'If you stay here and——'

'No... Apart from anything else I don't want to be any more——' She broke off abruptly.

'Beholden to me?' he suggested. 'Well, I'm afraid you'll have to be.' Brutally, he went on, 'Don't forget that until I say the word you haven't got a job to go to.' The threat was implicit.

'But you... you promised...'

'My recollection is that I promised nothing. I said, "I *may* advise that Mr Stanton take you on."'

'You said Cromford's needed someone who could draw with humour and imagination...' Swallowing, she added raggedly, 'I *have* to have a job.'

'Well, if you're prepared to be sensible...'

'By "sensible", you mean...?'

'I mean staying here until you're fully recovered.'

It was the last thing she wanted to do. She *hated* having to accept either his help or his hospitality, and she both resented and feared his power over her. But he held the whip-hand, as well he knew. The recession was biting deep, job opportunities were rare as snow in Florida, and unless she earned some money soon she'd be thrown out of her apartment. Then what would she do?

He watched the conflict on her expressive face and his lips twisted sardonically. 'I take it your precious pride's troubling you?'

That wasn't all by a long chalk, but it was all she was prepared to admit to. Making up her mind, she informed him stiltedly, 'I'll stay on for a few days so long as it's clearly understood that as soon as I'm earning you'll take back every penny I owe you.'

'Don't worry, when the time comes, I intend to exact full payment.'

His choice of phrase brought a warning prickle. A quick glance showed his expression was bland and appeared to hold no hint of intimidation. But, though his face was rarely impassive, she was well aware that normally it only revealed what he allowed it to, and she remained distinctly uneasy.

Yet it looked as if she had no alternative.

'Perhaps you could bring some of my day clothes, then?' Quickly Dita listed the items she thought she might need.

'Anything else?' he queried. She shook her head. He smiled briefly, and leaned forward as if intending to kiss her goodbye. Her thoughts, her heartbeat, her breathing, all seemed to stop, and she sat as if turned to stone, waiting for the touch of his lips. But after hesitating fractionally he drew back, and in a kind of daze she watched him turn and walk away and the bedroom door closed behind him.

How much of a fool could she be? she berated herself. Once she'd loved this man, craved his kisses, and it had almost destroyed her. Even now, when she both feared and mistrusted his motives and intentions, he still had a potent physical attraction that she found almost impossible to fight.

But fight it she must.

She felt on edge and jumpy, restless as a cat shut in the wrong house.

Lying down again, she willed herself to relax, but thoughts thronged her mind, making it busy as Times Square. Recalling her disquieting during-the-night conversation with Rider, she shivered.

It was disturbing, *shocking*, to think he really hated her. She didn't want to believe it. But his, 'What makes you doubt it?' and his accusing, 'You ran out on me,' seemed branded into her brain in letters of fire.

She shivered afresh and tried to tell herself that his admittedly melodramatic gloating, his, 'I'm keeping that for a surprise,' when she'd asked what he hoped to gain, had been only an attempt to scare her.

But *had* it?

Though respected for his fairness in business dealings, he was a ruthless man, a man who had been known to break anyone foolish enough to try and cheat or cross him.

Over the next couple of days, Dita made good headway. The illness-induced lethargy gradually left her, and when she went to the bathroom her legs began to feel less like chewed string.

After lunch each day she went downstairs and, with Mrs Merriton's blessing, spent a couple of hours on the settee reading or watching television, before going back to bed.

Rider hadn't returned from town, but the housekeeper said comfortably that he was keeping in touch by phone and would probably be home that weekend.

On Sunday afternoon, feeling much stronger, Dita got dressed and made her way down the elegant oak staircase and across the panelled hall to the sitting-room.

It had changed, in that indefinable way new surroundings did, and from being strange was now pleasantly familiar, with the firelight reflected in its polished sideboard and the stately tick-tock of its grandfather clock.

Having chosen a new paperback from the well-stocked bookcase, Dita put her feet up and settled herself on the settee. But the story failed to hold her interest and instead of reading she stared out of the window.

Snow still blanketed the Catskills, but according to the local news they had so far escaped lightly compared to the white-outs winter blizzards quite frequently brought to the area.

And it was beautiful, a wonderland of glistening trees and virgin snow, only the tracks of birds and animals marring the smooth white expanse. But in Manhattan it would be mud-spattered and nasty underfoot, with dirty slush edging the pavements.

Visualising town brought Dita's thoughts back to Rider. The weekend was almost over and still there was no sign of him. She told herself firmly that it was better if he did stay away, yet a traitorous part of her *wanted* him to come.

Right from the start her emotions had been chaotic where he was concerned. Only for a short time had she felt secure, sure and serene, her confidence engendered by the smile in his grey eyes and his softly spoken, 'I love you.'

But she hadn't known then that it was a false security, a mistaken confidence, and by the time she'd learnt the truth it was too late.

She felt a bleak desolation of spirit, a poignant sorrow that her short-lived happiness had been based on a fallacy. All at once she wanted to cry...

The sharp click of a latch scattered her thoughts the way a gunshot scattered starlings. She lifted her head dazedly to find the sitting-room had grown dusky and Rider was standing in the flickering firelight looking down at her.

Indifference was something she could never feel where this man was concerned, and her heart began to beat a rapid tattoo against her ribcage. 'You're home,' she said foolishly.

'How are you feeling?' he asked, studying her face.

'I'm fine now,' she assured him.

'But something's wrong?'

'No, nothing's wrong.'

'Then why are you crying?'

'I—I'm not crying,' she stammered.

He stooped to take her face between his hands, brushing his thumbs over the shiny tracks of wetness. 'Strange, that's what it looks like.'

She jerked away, and his hands fell to his sides. Sitting on the edge of the settee, his muscular thigh trapping her legs as though to punish her for that swift with-drawal, he suggested blandly, 'Perhaps you're worrying about Paul Wilson?'

His words were like an unexpected blow in the solar plexus. 'How do you know about Paul?' she gasped.

'While I was collecting some of your things I came across a letter from his mother.'

Furiously, she cried, 'You have no right to read my mail!'

Ignoring her anger, he said, 'I take it the boy was hurt in the same accident as your husband?'

After a second or two she admitted, 'Yes, he was. I...'
And it was all her fault.

Suddenly the unbearable guilt, the sadness, the futile regrets and bitter despair overflowed and she was sobbing. Sobs that tore her throat and chest and took more breath than she'd got. Since the accident she had never shed a single tear; now, as though a levee had collapsed and allowed a river to burst free, she couldn't stop.

No one with a spark of humanity could have witnessed such anguish unmoved. Leaning forward, Rider gathered her into his arms and held her close, one hand moving up and down her spine in a curiously soothing gesture until she was all cried out.

When the sobs were replaced by hiccuping gasps, he fished a spotless hankie from his pocket and mopped her up with a sort of wry tenderness.

Making an effort to pull herself together, she drew away and sat staring blindly into the fire. Allowing her no time to repair her defences, he urged, 'Tell me about it.'

As though under hypnosis, she obeyed. 'The Wilsons were returning from a family outing when Stephen's car hit their pick-up and both vehicles went off the road.' Her voice wavering, scarcely audible, she added, 'Mr and Mrs Wilson and their daughter escaped with minor injuries, but Paul was badly hurt and left crippled... He was their pride and joy...' Unable to go on, she stared down at her clenched hands.

'How old is he?' Rider asked.

Dita swallowed hard. 'Coming up to eleven.'

'Is he still confined to hospital?'

'No, he's home. But he needs special treatment, endless care and attention. The Wilsons do their level best, but they're a poor family. They don't have the money it takes to care adequately for a sick child, nor buy the appliances that would make all their lives so much easier.'

'I gather you help them as much as you can?'

'Yes, but I ...'

'You already have debts you can't settle.'

Flushing, vexed that he knew how bad her financial problems were, she lifted her chin and said hardily, 'All I need is a job... Please, Rider...' For Paul's sake, she was prepared to beg.

'Helping the Wilsons seems to be of overriding importance to you,' he remarked thoughtfully.

'It is.' Her voice had grown stronger and risen a little. 'That's why I *have* to have that job.'

He laughed harshly. 'As far as I can see, even with a well-paid job you've more than enough on your plate.'

'Well, now I've no hospital bills coming in, as soon as I'm earning I can at least make some kind of regular contribution.'

'But not enough.' He was brutally honest. 'I've been making a few careful enquiries and they need a great deal more financial assistance than you'll be in a position to give.'

'Why have you been making enquiries? It's not your affair.'

As though she hadn't spoken, he continued, 'I understand the child must have a wheelchair, among other things, if he's to get any proper schooling.'

'I know that,' she admitted hopelessly. The thought had haunted her often enough on the nights when sleep had refused to come. 'But at the moment I can't do anything about it.'

'*I* can.'

'No,' she cried sharply. 'It's none of your business. I won't allow you to give them money on my behalf.'

'Don't you want the child to be able to live as normal a life as possible?'

She stared at him, swollen eyes mirroring her pain and confusion. 'Of course I do.'

Rider dropped into an armchair opposite and continued in a businesslike tone, 'He'd have every opportunity if I made myself responsible for all his medical expenses.'

She swallowed hard. 'Why would you be prepared to do that?'

Hatefully mocking, he asked, 'You don't believe it's out of the goodness of my heart?'

'No. I think you've got an ulterior motive.'

'Hardly *ulterior*,' he objected. 'I made no secret of the fact that I wanted a hold over you.'

'But why do you want a hold over me? What do you *want*?' Her voice had risen and grown shrill with alarm.

She scarcely heard his soft answer, but she watched his lips frame the word, 'You.'

'You don't mean it,' she whispered.

'Oh, I mean it all right.'

'I don't believe this…' she muttered frantically. 'How *can* you expect me to sleep with you when my husband's only been dead a few weeks?'

'You must think I'm a complete swine.' Rider's voice was filled with bitterness.

She gazed at him, almost deafened by the beating of her own heart.

When she stayed silent, he went on, 'The deal is this… I'm prepared to start helping Paul's family immediately by giving them a regular monthly allowance and any further financial assistance they may require. In return I want you.' He paused deliberately. 'But I won't try to rush you. I'll let you have as much time as it takes, then——'

'Then you'll claim your pound of flesh,' she broke in bitterly.

'A picturesque way of putting it,' he commented.

Almost despairingly, she cried, 'The Wilsons are a decent family. If I told them the truth they wouldn't accept your help.'

He shrugged slightly. 'That's up to you. But somehow I don't think you will.'

'Suppose I just say no deal, nothing on earth would make me agree to your terms?'

His face was a bronze mask in the firelight. 'Then I've failed to get what I want.'

'And you want me for your mistress...'

'No,' he said evenly, 'my wife.'

While he got up to light one of the standard lamps and toss another couple of logs on the fire, she gaped at him speechless, hardly believing her ears.

It didn't make sense. If he wanted a wife, why hadn't he married Julie Dawn, the woman who'd been carrying his baby? And, no matter what he said now, there was no doubt it *was* his baby. He'd admitted as much...

There was a brisk tap at the door and Mrs Merriton came bustling in. She placed the tray she was carrying on a low table and, not seeming to notice the emotionally charged atmosphere, asked, 'Would you like a plate of brownies with your tea? Or would you prefer some English muffins?'

'Oh, muffins, I think,' Rider decided. 'And we'll toast our own over the fire.' He moved one of the logs aside, exposing the glowing red embers beneath, and when the housekeeper returned bringing the muffins he crouched on his haunches with a long-handled toasting fork.

As soon as the first one was golden-brown, he spread it liberally with butter and passed it to Dita.

Somehow she found her voice. 'Thank you, that looks delicious.'

'I thought the cat had got your tongue,' he remarked sardonically, as she bit into the hot, buttery round. 'Since I mentioned the word "wife" you haven't said a thing.'

She chewed and swallowed. 'Didn't you expect me to be surprised?'

'Not to the extent that it would rob you of speech.' He speared his own muffin and crouched to toast it. 'I'm nearly thirty-two. It's high time I got married and settled down to be a family man.'

His words brought a swift searing pain that made her want to hit back. 'If you're so keen to have a wife and children, why didn't you marry Julie Dawn?'

He glanced up, his grey eyes like flint. 'I'll give you two reasons among many. First, the baby wasn't mine, and I've a rooted objection to having another man's child foisted on me. Second, she didn't want marriage, all she wanted was a massive pay-off.'

A kind of painful curiosity made Dita ask, 'Did she get it?'

'No, she didn't. I managed to spike her guns.' Interpreting the look on Dita's face aright, he snapped, 'You've no need to feel sorry for her; she's not worth it, I assure you.'

'So I take your word for it?'

'It's a long story.' His voice was flat, with a quality of fatigue that seemed alien to him. 'One of these days I may tell you the whole of it.'

Though he probably never would, she realised. Rider was, in his own way, a very private man.

Indicating that the subject was closed, he advised brusquely, 'Finish your muffin before it gets cold.'

Having obeyed, she ventured tentatively, 'Rider...why do you want to marry me?'

His face full of mockery, he said, 'Don't you think it's high time you made an honest man of me?'

She moved her head, repudiating his levity. 'Are you really serious about wanting me to be your wife?'

Coming to squat by her side, he used the ball of his thumb to wipe a dribble of butter from her chin, before answering, 'Quite serious, Perdita. I knew I wanted to marry you the first day I walked into Tim Ryan's office and saw you sitting behind that desk so cool and prim.'

He rose to his feet and stood looking down at her. 'I intended to propose to you when I came back from San Francisco, but you'd vanished like a wraith, as if you'd never been a flesh-and-blood woman.' There was anger and pain and frustration in that taut statement.

Hands clenched into tight fists, Dita struggled to keep in check emotions too powerful to be easily controlled.

After a moment he went on bleakly, 'A long time ago I read somewhere that Perdita meant "lost lady". It seemed particularly applicable.' Suddenly his hands shot out and fastened on her shoulders, his fingers biting in, bruising the fragile bones. 'Why did you go?'

'You're hurting me,' she protested.

He shook her a little and, his voice full of anguish, repeated, 'Why?'

'I didn't fancy being part of a harem,' she spat at him. And wondered how it was that after all this time the concept still had the power to hurt so badly. 'I still don't,' she added.

As though he was making a positive effort, his grip loosened and fell away. 'You have my word that you are, and will be, the only woman in my life.'

She smiled without mirth. 'You told me that once before, remember?'

'It was true then, and it's true now.'

For a moment she was shaken by the absolute sincerity in his manner, then, because she *wanted* it to be the truth and knew it wasn't, she turned on him furi-

ously. 'You must take me for a complete fool. I read in
the paper about the confrontation at LaGuardia. You
admitted you were Julie Dawn's lover. And don't try to
tell me the Press made *that* up.'

'No, they didn't make it up,' he confirmed heavily. 'It
was a gamble on my part.' His laugh was mirthless,
brittle, full of pain. 'I staked everything on you trusting
me. Though you'd never said so, I was foolish enough
to believe you loved me——'

'I did love you,' she broke in hotly.

'But you didn't trust me.'

'How *could* I trust you?'

'There's no love—at least, not the kind of love *I*
want—without trust. So, having failed to find that, I'll
give up on love and settle for reparation.'

'But you can't want a forced marriage,' she cried.

'Hardly forced.' His face was stony. 'You have a
choice.'

But she hadn't. She was trapped and she knew it. There
was no way she could bring herself to deprive Paul's
family of the help they so desperately needed.

White to the lips, she said, 'You know quite well I
haven't... And, no matter how you dress it up or try
to disguise the truth, a forced marriage is what it will
amount to.'

'So be it,' he accorded curtly. 'Though I venture to
suggest that you won't find it *such* a hardship to share
my bed.'

'Then why do I feel as if I'm facing a death sentence?'

'I really can't imagine. If my memory serves me cor-
rectly, you were a very willing partner.' He smiled,
taunting her with past knowledge. 'In fact I recall being
stunned by the fire and passion of your somewhat un-
tutored response.'

Flushing hotly, she cursed herself for not holding her tongue.

'Well?' he pressed, when she remained silent. 'Do we have a bargain?'

Swallowing hard, she stated, 'On one condition.'

'Name it.'

'That I work, retain my independence.'

Scowling, he objected, 'There'll be no need for you to work.'

'I *want* to,' she insisted. 'I want that job at Cromford's. I've no intention of letting you support me.'

His eyes narrowed. 'Still the same old pride.'

'It's all I've got left,' she flared with sudden bitterness.

'Very well, I agree to your terms... With one condition.'

'Name it.'

'*Touché.*' He acknowledged the aptness of her retort. 'The condition is this—that when you leave here you move into Markman's.'

As she began to shake her head vehemently, he added curtly, 'I'm not suggesting you move in with me. I shall arrange a room for you in the hotel proper.'

One of the older Grand Hotels, Markman's was famous for its massive foyer, the huge fireplaces filled with flowers in the summer and log fires in the winter, and also for the care it lavished on its guests. The place had a friendly, almost old-fashioned atmosphere which was pleasant and homely. But the cost of a room there would be way beyond her means.

She shook her head. 'I've no intention of living in a hotel. When I leave here I'm going back to Gooker Street.'

'You can't go back to Gooker Street,' he stated unequivocally. 'When I went up to collect your things the landlord appeared and informed me he'd already let the apartment to someone else. So, you see, you'll have to find another place to live.'

When she'd absorbed the blow, she objected, 'But I need to stay somewhere cheaper than Markman's.'

He sighed. 'Not all the rooms are expensive, and as I happen to own the place...'

'You do?' For a moment she was surprised, though, thinking about it, she didn't know why. She'd always been aware that he owned a great deal of property in New York and other major cities.

Reluctantly, she agreed, 'Well, I'll stay for a week or two until I can find somewhere else. But in the meantime I insist on paying the proper rent.'

He gritted his teeth. 'You are the most stubborn...' Suddenly he stopped and, studying her pale, spent face swore softly. 'I'm an absolute idiot. You look exhausted. I should have taken you back to bed an hour ago.'

Before she could make any protest, he scooped her into his arms and carried her upstairs. She was aware of solid bone and muscle, the hard strength of him, and her heart began to race with suffocating speed as she faced the unwelcome realisation of her own need.

He turned his head a little and grey eyes looked into green. As though the years apart had just served to concentrate and refine it, she knew that the attraction which had drawn them together in the first place was more potent than ever.

As though he too felt its disturbing effects, he put her down and walked away with an abrupt, 'Goodnight, Perdita.'

But it was more than mere attraction, she admitted, lying awake and restless in the big bed. Though she was trying hard to fight it, he dominated her mind, her thoughts, her feelings.

After everything that had happened the knowledge that she was still held in thrall came as a shock. But it shouldn't have done. She had felt it from their very first meeting, this powerful enslavement of both spirit and senses.

Perhaps a simpler word for it was love.

But how *could* she continue to love a man she couldn't trust, who had lied to her and ruined her life? Yet she *did*.

Fool! fool! she berated herself. Nothing could be more stupid, more dangerous than to feel this way about a man who had admitted hating her, who only wanted reparation. A man who had deliberately trapped her into agreeing to what would undoubtedly be an empty, soul-destroying mockery of a marriage.

CHAPTER FOUR

By THE time Dita awoke the next morning Rider had already left for town, and it was almost midday on Saturday before he returned.

It had seemed a long, strangely lonely week.

When she heard his light step crossing the hall excitement brought her to her feet, and it was as much as she could do not to fly to meet him. But by the time he appeared in the doorway she had donned an abstracted expression and was to all intents and purposes deep in a biography of Abraham Lincoln.

'How are you, Perdita?' Rider greeted her with a cool reserve that was at variance with her own inward rush of pleasure.

'I'm fine now, thank you.' She answered like a well-mannered child.

He gave her an unsparing appraisal. 'You certainly look much better.'

'Oh, I am. There's really no reason for me to stay here any longer.' The words came out in a rush.

Rider's hard mouth took on a wry slant and his gaze held hers. She disentangled it and, flustered, looked away, wishing she'd sounded a shade more gracious.

Well aware of her discomfort, he asked, 'So how soon would you like to leave?'

Flushing a little, she said stiffly, 'As soon as it's convenient.'

'Then shall we say straight after lunch?'

'I . . . I have got a room?'

His grey eyes wary, he replied, 'I realised it would be expensive for you to keep eating out, so I've arranged for you to have a small, self-contained apartment.'

'I can't possibly afford an apartment,' she objected.

In a long-suffering voice he asked, 'How do you know before I tell you how much it is?'

'All right, how much is it?'

He named an amount that was far from cheap, but quite modest by New York standards, adding, 'The place has been standing empty for a week or so.'

'Why hasn't it been in use?' she demanded sceptically.

'It's in need of redecoration.'

She bit her lip. Whether that was the truth or not, she'd have to accept it and move in for a short while at least.

After lunch, when she had thanked the housekeeper warmly for all her care, bringing a flush of pleasure to that lady's sallow face with an impulsive hug, they made a start.

Although Dita was more than ready to take up the reins again, she left Rider's Keep with a strange feeling of regret.

Midweek a spell of mild, bright weather had cleared the snow, but now it had turned cold again. A biting wind ruffled the dark green pines, and a moving black tracery of bare branches was etched against a sky of icy pearl.

The early part of the drive was spectacular, but her eyes were more often on Rider's strong profile than the passing scenery. He looked tired, she thought, as though he had been pushing himself to the limit and beyond.

Unbidden, a feeling of tenderness that was almost maternal made her want to cradle his fair head against her breast. Idiot! she berated herself. She must never forget that he was a tough, ruthless man, at his most dangerous when he appeared vulnerable.

For a while he drove without speaking, then began somewhat abruptly, 'I've had the usual formalities waived, so if you're feeling up to it you can start at Cromford's on Monday.' He slanted her a look. 'Unless, of course, you've changed your mind?'

'No, I haven't changed my mind.'

'Do you know any details?' he queried.

She shook her head. 'No.' Details were something she hadn't got round to worrying about.

He told her the hours she would be expected to work and what her salary would be. It was considerably more than she'd anticipated.

After a quick glance at her face he said crisply, 'There's no need to look so suspicious. That's the rate for the job.'

Dita let her breath out in a faint sigh of relief. With that amount coming in, it should be possible to make a start on her pile of bills and pay the rent she owed.

Only when Rider said succinctly, 'It's already paid,' did she realise she'd spoken the thought aloud. 'And before you explode with righteous indignation,' he added sardonically, 'I had to give your landlord a cheque before he'd release your belongings.'

'In that case I'll pay you as soon as possible,' she said spiritedly. The devilish glint in his eye made her hurriedly rephrase that. 'I mean I'll give you the money back as soon as I can.'

His crooked smile told her she'd fallen for his deliberate baiting. Lips pursed, she turned to stare resolutely out of the window until the New Jersey sprawl gave way to the familiar skyline of Manhattan.

Having garaged the car and picked up her keys from the reception desk in Markman's foyer, Rider escorted her into the lift. All the hotel staff had a smile and a respectful greeting for him, and Dita noted that the smiles and greetings were returned. Whatever his faults, he was certainly no snob, she admitted.

Her apartment proved to be a small corner suite immediately beneath the penthouse. When Rider had unlocked the door, he gave her the keys, saying, 'These are yours to keep; you don't need to hand them in when you go out.'

There was an attractive sitting-room, with a wonderful view over Central Park and side-windows which looked along the length of Fifth Avenue, and a single bedroom with an *en-suite* bathroom. If it was in need of decoration it certainly wasn't evident.

Warm and comfortable and *homely*, it was a far cry from Gooker Street.

Indicating the walk-in wardrobes that lined one wall, he remarked, 'You'll find that the rest of your clothes and other belongings I collected have been unpacked and put away.'

The kitchen was tiny, but nicely equipped, and a look around showed full cupboards and a well-stocked fridge and freezer.

'All the normal cleaning and servicing will be done unless you give instructions to the contrary,' Rider told her, 'and there's a twenty-four-hour room service, so until you feel up to cooking for yourself just send down for anything you want.' Grey eyes gleaming mockingly, he added, 'They have a cheap rate for semi-permanent residents.'

Hanging on to her composure, she said, 'Really?'

'Really.' His voice was dry.

When she followed him back into the living-room, he remarked, 'By the way, I've opened a bank account for you.' Seeing she was about to protest, he held up a restraining hand. 'Just a modest sum until your salary cheque is paid in. If there's anything else you need you only have to ask.'

'Thank you.' Far from happy at being forced to accept his help, she found it almost impossible to sound gracious.

The irony in his grey eyes told her he knew her feelings exactly. Glancing at his watch, he remarked, 'This seems to be a suitable time to try out the room service, unless you'd like to join me for dinner in the penthouse...?'

She was already shaking her head.

'Then I'll ask them to send a meal up here before I leave you to settle in.'

His phrasing was a little ambiguous, making her ask, 'Are you staying to eat with me?'

Rider's eyes met and held hers and a flame seemed to spring into life between them. While she stood as though paralysed, his warm palms came up to frame her face and his look became intense, searching. 'Do you want me to, Perdita?' Her name was thick and sweet as honey on his tongue.

Her heart suddenly racing, she stared up into those clear grey eyes and longed to press her body to the warmth and strength of his, to feel his mouth close over hers...

All at once guilt doused the flame like a jet of icy water, and she jerked away as though contaminated by his touch.

Rider's hands dropped and his jaw clenched. A white line etched around his mouth, the bones in his face sharply delineated beneath the taut skin, he said furiously, 'Don't bother to answer that,' and headed for the door.

Somehow she found her voice. 'Rider... I didn't mean to... Please don't go...'

He turned to look at her, his eyes bleak as a winter dawn, unmoved by her stumbling words. 'I had the distinct impression that my touch was offensive, to say the least, that you couldn't wait to be rid of me.'

'No, no... I just...'

'Why bother to lie about it? After all, our agreement specified as much time as you need to adjust.' A second later the door closed quietly behind him.

She stood absolutely still, blinking back tears. Despite everything she had quite desperately wanted him to stay.

Over the next weeks, apart from an occasional accidental meeting in the lift, or by the hotel pool, where they exchanged a few words with the wary civility of strangers, she saw little of Rider.

Though she guessed he monitored her every move, he never came to her door or sought her out, and she wondered if he was still nursing his anger, or just being scrupulous in giving her the time he'd promised.

She received a letter from Mrs Wilson that was overflowing with joy and gratitude, beginning, 'I don't know how to thank you or your future husband. You can't imagine what a difference this help has already made to all our lives...' and ending, 'God bless you both.'

Some of the burden of guilt was lifted from her soul, and, though she hadn't yet started to count the cost, she felt happier than she'd felt since the accident.

Still with very mixed feelings as far as Rider was concerned, she made a conscious decision to cope with the present and not worry about the future.

While the trees budded and daffodils and jonquils began to dance in Central Park, she put on six pounds of badly needed weight, and, having recovered her energy, finished off the private commissions she'd been working on when she took ill.

At first she made a determined effort to find other accommodation, but it was as difficult as trying to find a gold needle in a haystack and gradually she stopped looking.

Once she'd settled in at Cromford's she found a kind of stability and a whole new sense of identity. The work was varied and exciting and her colleagues were a cheerful, friendly bunch who, without prying into her private life, treated her as one of the crowd.

She made a point of walking to work to save bus fares and generally lived as frugally as possible. From time to time, when she'd amassed a little money, she pushed a cheque beneath Rider's door.

Her apartment became home, and when the staff at Markman's started to greet her by name and smile as though they were genuinely pleased to see her some of the ice around her heart melted and she was conscious of a feeling of warmth, a sensation of belonging.

Rider spent most of his weekends in the Catskills, but he never asked her to accompany him, and, though she would have liked to, she was too proud to suggest it.

In the spare time she now seemed to have a good deal of, Dita began writing again, humorous fairy-stories which she illustrated herself. But she was living from day to day in a kind of time capsule, still afraid to look either back to the past or forward to the future.

Then, showing how fast the year was flying, summer arrived, filling the canyons of Manhattan with dust and heat and the parks with half-naked bodies and picnic litter. Sandals and shorts ousted more formal wear, while sunhats came out in force.

It was a sunny Saturday morning in July and Dita was returning from a pre-breakfast walk by Central Park lake, when George Carter, a cheerful elderly man who had just come on desk duty, greeted her with a beaming smile and handed her a letter.

As soon as she'd let herself into her apartment and measured coffee and water into the glass jug, she tore open the envelope and read with a pleasurable surge of excitement that her book of children's stories had been accepted for publication.

She was still hugging the news to her when there was a tap at the door. A smile on her lips, she switched off the bubbling percolator and went to answer.

To her surprise, Rider stood there, tall and wide-shouldered, casually clothed, his thick fair hair a little damp as though he'd recently showered or been swimming in the pool.

Wondering why he'd come, trying to hide the sudden gladness just seeing him caused, Dita forced herself to say steadily, 'Hello stranger. Come on in. There's some freshly made coffee if you'd like a cup?'

He followed her into the kitchen and accepted a cup of black coffee, leaning negligently against the cupboards to drink it. There was a constraint between them, on his part a deliberate holding back, on hers an emotional frustration that tied her tongue.

Powerfully aware of his attraction, she looked anywhere but at him, busying herself fitting slices of rye bread into the toaster.

Evenly, he said, 'The last cheque you pushed under my door more than covers your rent arrears and your board and lodging at the Keep. I admire your determination to be independent for as long as possible, but enough is enough, Perdita.'

Grey eyes met green in a silent clash of wills from which Rider emerged the undoubted victor.

When her eyes fell, apparently satisfied, he felt in his pocket and produced a letter. 'This came earlier. I thought you might like to read it.'

From Mrs Wilson, and addressed to them jointly, it first gave details of Paul's progress at school, then went on, '...and the special equipment you paid for is making his life so much easier... But the best news of all is that the extra physiotherapy is having *wonderful* results and giving cause for real hope that one day he will walk again...'

While Dita deciphered the small, cramped writing, Rider helped himself to more coffee. When she'd finished reading, relief and gladness swelling inside her, she smiled at him warmly. 'Thank you, you're very kind.'

A hard flush appeared along his cheekbones. Caustically, he said, 'I'm only keeping my part of the bargain. So long as you keep yours, there's no need for spurious gratitude.'

Her thanks had been genuine and spontaneous, and his response came as a shock. Anger embraced her and, welcoming it like an old friend, she lashed out at him verbally, 'I have every intention of keeping my half of the bargain, but I was brought up to have good manners... Though I could wish I hadn't bothered to say thank you when you're being so rude and arrogant and downright obnoxious...'

Without a word he swung on his heel and strode towards the door.

Her anger draining away like water down a plug-hole, she ran after him and caught his arm. 'Rider... Don't go... Please don't go...'

He stopped and turned to face her, his eyes wintry, a grim set to his beautiful mouth.

'I'm sorry,' she whispered, the green eyes raised to his luminous with tears.

His expression softened and he admitted, 'I'm the one who should be sorry. Forgive me, Perdita?'

She pursed her lips as though considering the matter, then said boldly, 'I might, if you take me out to dinner tonight.'

A strange look flitted across his face. 'I'm afraid I can't make it tonight. Will tomorrow night do?'

'Of course,' she agreed lightly.

'Then I'll call for you about seven.'

As she watched his broad back disappear down the corridor she wondered why he couldn't make it tonight. Was he meeting some other woman? Julie Dawn, for instance?

If he was, she couldn't really blame him. Admittedly he'd promised *she* would be the only woman in his life, but for months they had been virtual strangers and no red-blooded man could be expected to live like a monk indefinitely.

But, in spite of all her attempts at rationalisation, she felt hurt and angry and miserably jealous.

After the next evening, as though the ice was broken, he began to take her out once or twice a week. On each occasion he made a marvellous companion, and she felt all the old magic and excitement, but to her secret chagrin he treated her like a sister.

Autumn blew in early, chasing discarded newspapers and sweet wrappers along Wall Street, pouncing on canopies and awnings, tearing gold and scarlet confetti from the trees and showering it down like a ticker-tape welcome to autumn.

Outdoor skaters at the Rockefeller Center began to don scarves and woollen hats; on street corners golden corn cobs turned black over glowing braziers, and the seasonal smell of roasting chestnuts filled the air.

Open fires blazed cheerfully in Markman's huge foyer and, regardless of the central heating, men stood with their backs to them in traditional stance, while women warmed their hands at the flames.

It was then that Dita realised she was whole again, able to leave the past where it belonged and face the future. But, though she was convinced that Rider no longer hated her, his true feelings were a mystery, making their future together, any chance of happiness, uncertain, to say the least.

She knew her returning smile and the sparkle in her eyes must have told him more plainly than words that her mourning was finally over, but still he made no move.

One evening in late October, feeling unsettled and restless, she was standing by her window at dusk staring out at a beautiful plum and charcoal sky, when a disturbing thought occurred to her: had Rider changed his mind about making her his wife?

It would be ironic if he had when she now knew that, in spite of all the risks, that was what she wanted more than anything else in the world.

But even if he hadn't changed his mind there was a stumbling-block, something she had to confess before she could marry him. And when he knew how things stood he might not want to go through with it.

If he *did*, she wouldn't let the guilt she still felt over Stephen's death come between them, Dita resolved, and she would do her utmost to make their marriage work.

She sighed, her breath misting on the glass. So all she had to do now was wait with what patience she could command until he broached the subject.

Then suddenly, with a blinding flash of insight, she knew he never would. Too proud to approach her, inhibited by the fact that he'd used coercion, he was waiting for *her* to make the first move.

Having slept badly that night, Dita got up next morning with a slight headache and a set determination to have things out and know precisely where she stood.

She was on her way to the kitchen to make some coffee when she noticed the white oblong envelope which had been pushed under her door.

It bore her name in Rider's strong, left-handed scrawl. The note inside was short and to the point.

By the time you read this I'll be on a flight to London. I expect to be in Europe for at least a fortnight on business. Please feel free to use the money in your account. Take care of yourself. R.

Her first stunned disbelief turned to fury. When he'd taken her out for dinner a couple of nights ago, though he'd talked about his work for a fair part of the time, he hadn't so much as mentioned a trip.

Green eyes sparkling angrily, she crumpled the note into a ball and threw it across the kitchen. Damn him. Damn him! His meaning couldn't have been plainer. He was leaving the coast clear, giving her every opportunity to disappear again.

This conclusion was backed to the hilt when later that morning she checked her bank balance and found it exceeded fifty thousand dollars.

After a great deal of serious thought she felt convinced that it wasn't because he *wanted* her to go, but because a fine sense of guilt that he'd put her in the position she was in made it necessary to give her the chance.

Having settled that to her satisfaction, she rang his secretary to check the exact date of his return, then waited with what patience she could muster for the time to pass.

A few days before he was due back, she went into the bank and withdrew the bulk of her money in the form of a cheque made out to him.

On the following Friday, having asked permission in advance, Dita left work early and hurried back to Markman's. Anger steeling her, she went up to her apartment and, putting the keys and her depleted bank book in an envelope, slipped them under Rider's door before going down to the lobby again.

Making her way to the desk, where George was on duty, she asked, 'Will you do me a big favour...? Mr Barron's due home quite shortly. Can you liaise with the car-park attendant and let me know the exact time of his arrival?'

'Consider it done.'

'George, you're an absolute darling.' Dita's smile left a blushing George her slave for life.

It was a bare half-hour before her phone rang and she learnt that Rider was on his way up. She gave him ten minutes, then, taking a slip of paper from a drawer, she braced herself and made her way to the penthouse.

Her heart beating in great heavy thuds, she opened the door without knocking and walked in. He was sitting staring into space, such sadness and desolation written on his face that she caught her breath.

He glanced up sharply and froze, then the look of anguish vanished and his features settled into a carved mask. 'Well, well...' he said softly. 'I hardly expected to see you.'

'What did you expect? That I'd take your money and run? Well, thanks, but no, thanks.' She thrust the cheque at him and, her temper rising, went on, 'Though you certainly did your best to make it easy for me.'

'You don't sound particularly grateful,' he observed mildly.

'I'm not grateful, I'm furious! You once accused me of not trusting you. How much did *you* trust *me*? You really believed I'd gone!'

Indicating the bank book and keys, he asked, 'Isn't that what you intended me to believe?'

'Yes.'

'May I ask why?'

'I wanted to pay you back,' she admitted.

His laugh was harsh. 'An eye for an eye and a tooth for a tooth?'

She bent the quotation a little. 'Great is justice and mighty above all things.'

'*Touché.*' He acknowledged her riposte.

When he said nothing further, she stated, 'We made a bargain. You've kept your half...'

He asked mockingly, 'And you plan to keep yours?' Aware that, for a variety of reasons, she couldn't tell him the truth about her feelings, she answered carefully, 'Yes. If you still want me to.'

'And if I say I don't?'

Realising she'd made a mistake, she said bravely, 'I wouldn't believe you.'

'Suppose I admit that the bargain should never have been struck in the first place?'

'But it *was.*' Seeing he was about to nullify it, she rushed into speech. 'And let's get one thing quite straight—I don't welsh on my bargains. You've kept your part, I have every intention of keeping mine.'

'The sacrificial lamb,' he jeered.

'Not on your life,' she shot back. 'I've no intention of being either a sacrifice or a lamb. Now I've found out what it's like to be grindingly poor, I rather fancy a rich husband. Especially one who's good in bed.'

Eyes glinting dangerously, he rose to his feet, seeming to tower over her. 'Perhaps you'd like to check out that last statement?'

Falling back a step or two despite all her efforts not to, she said offhandedly, 'There's really no need. I've got a good memory.'

'So have I.' His smile was disturbing. 'Good enough to remind me exactly what I've been missing. So suppose we clinch the bargain now?' He advanced on her with that lithe feline grace she always found so fascinating and so intimidating.

Well aware that he expected her to turn tail and run, she looked him in the eye and stood her ground until he loomed over her once more.

Reaching out, he spread lean fingers under the swell of her left breast. 'Your heart's racing.' His words held a mocking challenge.

She slid her hand inside his jacket and through the thin silky material of his shirt felt the strong beat quickening beneath her palm. 'So's yours.'

His fingers stayed in place but his thumb began to stroke over the soft curve, making the sensitive nipple firm beneath his touch. He made no move to kiss her, merely watched her reaction like a hawk.

A kind of mulish pride prevented her protesting, but, feeling like some specimen squirming on the end of a cruel pin, her face flamed with colour and her hand dropped to her side.

'Pity,' he drawled. 'I was rather hoping this tit for tat would continue. It opened up exciting possibilities. And seeing you cited good sex as one of your reasons for marrying me...'

She bit her lip.

Noting the small, betraying movement, he smiled sardonically. '...I shall expect a great deal of co-operation. Come.' He went into the bedroom, leaving her to follow.

She hesitated, wondering whether he was just testing her. This cold, clinical approach was quite different from what she'd anticipated. If only he'd take her in his arms, kiss her, she thought frantically. But for some reason he seemed to be intent on punishing her, humiliating her...

'Changed your mind?' he asked from the doorway.

'No.' Lifting her chin disdainfully, she joined him in the bedroom.

CHAPTER FIVE

RIDER closed the door behind her and, hands thrust nonchalantly into his pockets, legs crossed at the ankles, leaned broad shoulders against the panels, effectively cutting off any possible retreat.

His lean face was tanned and his thick blond hair, which he'd allowed to grow longer than usual, curled a little into his neck. He'd discarded his jacket and tie and undone the top two buttons of his ivory silk shirt, exposing the strong column of his throat.

An arrogant tilt to his head, his grey eyes brilliant between half-closed lids, he looked her over in insolent silence.

Feeling like some slave girl to be auctioned, she held on to her composure with an effort.

'Well?' he asked after a moment or two.

'Well what?' She refused to give an inch.

'Suppose you get undressed?'

'You first.'

He smiled thinly, and, never taking his eyes off her, began slowly to unbutton his shirt. Straightening up, he pulled it out of his waistband and, shrugging free of it, threw it to one side, exposing a healthily tanned chest and muscular shoulders. His movements beautifully co-ordinated, his shoes and socks followed.

Her mouth went dry as his fingers expertly dealt with the fastening of his trousers, and she watched in breathless fascination as he slid them over lean hips and stepped out of them. Even before he removed his striped silk briefs his arousal was evident.

Standing tall and supremely confident, long, well-shaped legs slightly apart, he waited.

Trying to ignore the treacherous flare of heat in her own abdomen, Dita began to take off her neat business suit with shaking hands, awkward and fumbling where he'd been easy and graceful. But when she was naked, though her face glowed scarlet as a poppy, she stood erect, head high, and stared back at him haughtily.

His smile full of mockery, he applauded. 'I must say, while you're in this frame of mind life is going to be far from dull.'

It took every ounce of will-power not to throw in the towel and beg for some sign of warmth, some kindness. She was only flaying herself; there was no way she could win this sexual battle. But, having started it, her stubborn spirit was reluctant to admit defeat.

'Aren't you going to lie down?' he enquired silkily, when she continued to stand there.

A fine dew sprang out on her temples and shivers ran over her skin, chilling it in spite of the carefully controlled air-conditioning. There was no way she could spread-eagle herself for his cool inspection. She must either give in or take the initiative.

Deciding on the latter, she walked towards him and, putting both hands flat against the warmth of his chest, leaned forward to brush her lips across the smooth golden skin of his collarbone. Though he remained motionless, his breathing and heart-rate quickened perceptibly.

She slid her arms around his neck and moved closer so that their bodies just brushed, and, standing on tiptoe, pressed an open-mouthed kiss against his throat. Feeling with triumph the shudder that ran through him, she bit him delicately.

His superb control broke, and with a muttered oath he hauled her hard against him and covered her mouth with his. It was the reaction she'd hoped for, and more, as he kissed her with such savage hunger that she ought to have been afraid.

But she wasn't.

He was her man, her mate, her love. With complete abandon she met and matched his ardour, giving him kiss for kiss, holding nothing back.

When he carried her to the bed and laid her down, arms locked tightly around his neck, she held on to him like life itself. With neither in any mood for preliminaries, their lovemaking was swift and fierce, consuming them both in the red-hot flames of passion and burnt boats.

Completely shattered, her heart pounding, her breath still coming in gasps, Dita lay with her eyes shut while he lifted himself away. She waited for him to draw her close, to cradle her head against his chest as he had done once before, but after a moment she felt the mattress dip then lift as he left the bed. A second or two later the bathroom door opened and closed and the shower started to run.

Her body still sang with the pleasure he'd given it, but her heart shed tears of blood. She'd taunted him with being good in bed, made it sound as if sex was all she wanted. Now it appeared that sex was all she was going to get.

But after seeing his face when he thought she'd gone she couldn't believe that all he felt for her was lust. There *had* to be something deeper, stronger. Even if it wasn't love.

She was sitting on the edge of the bed, a sheet pulled around her, when he emerged from the bathroom splendidly naked. His clear skin gleaming like oiled silk, he took clean briefs from one drawer and a casual shirt from another. It wasn't until he half turned that she saw the angry scratches scoring his back.

He heard her sharp intake of breath and smiled with what seemed to be a genuine amusement. 'Well, you did warn me you were no lamb. I just hadn't expected the tigress.'

'I'm sorry,' she whispered.

'There's no need to be. I'm quite looking forward to reaping the benefit of your experience.' Seeing her look blank, puzzled, a razor-sharp edge to his voice, he added, 'Someone's taught you a great deal since our last encounter.'

Clenching her teeth on the quick denial, she asked with bland politeness, 'May I use your shower?'

'Please do,' he answered, equally smooth and polite. 'Then perhaps you'd care to join me for dinner?' But suddenly there was an aloofness about him like a barbed-wire fence that was meant to keep her at a distance.

Finding her whole body was tender, and in places her flesh bore the signs of Rider's unbridled passion, she took her time, letting the hot water cascade soothingly over her while her thoughts moved uneasily.

Had she been wrong to precipitate this showdown? she wondered. The outcome certainly hadn't been what she'd planned, and seemed to have left them further apart than ever.

Having rubbed her long black hair until it was practically dry and borrowed a comb to pull through it, Dita emerged to find Rider had made use of her apartment keys, and fresh undies and a casual skirt and jumper were hanging over the back of a chair.

When she'd dressed and gathered together the clothes she'd discarded earlier, she ventured into the living-room to find that an oval table-trolley set with dinner for two had just been brought up. Three tall gold candles provided the only illumination, and the slatted blinds were drawn back to show a clear, star-spangled sky.

Rider came to meet her, his expression cool, slightly aloof, giving nothing away, and she wondered what he was thinking, feeling.

Though by now she knew him well, he was still in many ways an enigma. Even his physical appearance implied complexity, his lean body powerful yet supple, his mouth both sensual and fastidious, his hands strong but sensitive.

Impulsively she asked, 'Rider, do you regret what...what's just happened?'

Lips twisting, he said wryly, 'That's like asking a starving man if he regrets wolfing down a tempting meal... No, I can't regret what happened...only the *way* it happened.'

Biting her lip, she admitted that that had been her fault. *She* had forced the confrontation.

'Do *you* regret it, Perdita?'

His question brought her head up. Colour coming into her cheeks, she admitted, 'Yes, but it's a bit late now for regrets.'

A spasm of something that might have been torment crossed his face, only to be instantly wiped away, leaving just a handsome mask.

Having seated her, he filled both their glasses with a delicate white wine from the Napa Valley, and served her with Maine lobster and melted butter.

Head bent, candlelight casting the shadows of her long dark lashes on to her cheeks, she ate in silence. He made no attempt to break that silence but she was aware that he watched her constantly, while tension stretched between them like invisible wires.

When she refused the proffered cheese, he pushed it to one side and poured coffee for them both.

Unable to stand his unnerving scrutiny a moment longer, Dita picked up her cup and moved to one of the low armchairs drawn up in front of the sliding glass panels that led to the terrace and the roof-garden.

After a moment or two Rider followed and stood drinking his coffee while he stared out of the window at the twinkling lights and spectacular panorama that was night-time Manhattan.

Without turning, in a formal, businesslike tone, he queried, 'Do you still want to go through with this marriage?'

Wondering what *he* wanted, she hesitated just a fraction too long.

Swinging round, he asked bitingly, 'Or did I totally fail to come up to expectations?'

Ignoring his caustic question, and avoiding his eyes, she said firmly, 'Yes, I do want to go through with it.'

'Then I suggest we get married without too much delay...say, the twentieth?'

Knowing the time had come to tell him what she *must*, she put her cup down on the coffee-table with a little crash, and said, 'Before we go any further there's something I have to talk to you about.'

Picking up the desperation in her manner, he waited, every muscle taut. Candlelight gleamed in his eyes and hollowed his cheeks, highlighted his strong nose and shadowed his mouth. The contrast, striking in itself, helped to emphasise the combination of strength and sensitivity in his fascinating face.

Dita drew a deep, calming breath and let it out slowly. 'You once mentioned you would like to have children...a family.'

'Yes, I would... Wouldn't you?'

Though she tried to speak, no sound came.

'What's the matter, Perdita? Do you hate the thought of having my babies?'

She bit her inner lip until the blood ran warm and salty, hoping the small pain would make the bigger more bearable. Then, her voice barely above a whisper, she managed, 'I was pregnant once...when I was first married...'

He stood as though turned to marble, his face set in lines of shock and disbelief.

'I lost my baby at eleven weeks.'

His normally attractive voice oddly discordant, he asked, 'And you'd be afraid to try again?'

'No, it's not that. There were some...problems and the doctors told me I might not be able to conceive again. I'm sorry. I should have told you when you first mentioned marriage, but I...I hate having to talk about it.'

When he was silent, she forced herself to say, 'If this alters things, if you don't want to take the risk I...I'll quite understand.'

Though it could only have been a second or two, it seemed an eternity while she waited for his answer. When it came it was quite categorical. 'You are the only woman I want for my wife...'

She closed her eyes briefly in a prayer of thanksgiving.

'If we can't have children of our own I'm quite prepared to adopt some. Unless you object to the idea?'

'No... No, I don't. But they wouldn't be your own flesh and blood,' she pointed out shakily.

'Having you for my wife is more important.' Once again it was unequivocal.

Though in the dim light his handsome face showed nothing but a steely determination, she wondered again if it was possible that he loved her? If he could be so *certain*, surely he must care a little?

Carefully, trying her hardest to keep her voice level, she asked, '*Why* is it?'

'You've become an obsession, Perdita.'

The words held a savage bitterness that shocked her and made something that felt like an iron fist tighten around her heart. She took a deep, painful breath. 'I'm not sure I like the sound of that. Obsessions can be . . . unhealthy.'

' "Hope deferred maketh the heart sick" ,' he quoted with a crooked grin. 'Maybe once we're married, when you're in my bed every night and I can sate myself with you, my obsession will disappear.'

She shuddered, hating the way he'd phrased his remark, and wondering miserably if his obsession for her *did* disappear, what would there be to take its place? Boredom? Emptiness? Downright enmity?

Yet changing her mind was unthinkable. It was far too late. She was his body and soul and there was nothing for it but to go ahead and take a gamble on what the future might hold.

Watching the emotions chase across her face, he asked ironically, 'Decided to chance my turning into some kind of madman and locking you away in an ivory tower?'

She gave a little humourless smile. 'I think your penthouse is as close to an ivory tower as I'm ever likely to get. And yes, I'm ready to chance it.'

'Then shall we say the twentieth?'

'All right,' she agreed. 'The twentieth.'

'That way we'll be able to honeymoon over Christmas and New Year,' he added.

'Honeymoon?' She couldn't hide her dismay. With so many memories of failure and guilt, the last thing she wanted was a honeymoon.

'It's usual.' His voice grew rough and jeering. 'A time for soft lights, sweet music, and romance, not to mention love. Didn't you enjoy that euphoric start to marriage last time?'

All at once she was on dangerous ground. Stiffly she answered, 'No,' the way he'd phrased the question making her reply a truthful one. Unconsciously twisting her hands together, she added almost beseechingly, 'We don't really need a honeymoon, do we?'

His response was uncompromising. 'Yes, I rather think we do.' Though his face showed nothing of his feelings, she could sense his anger. After a moment, he queried, 'Is there anyone you want to ask to the wedding?'

Dita shook her head. 'Not really. Mrs Merriton, perhaps?'

'So no guests as such, only the minister and a couple of witnesses.'

'Surely you'll invite your parents?'

His face darkened. 'They're living in Washington, DC now. They may not want to come.'

She was well aware that there had never been any love lost between Rider and his father, but she'd always thought he liked his stepmother. Recalling how nice Kate Barron had always been to her, Dita persisted. 'I think you should at least give them the chance.'

Brusquely, he agreed, 'Very well, if you insist.'

'I don't insist,' she said quietly. 'But it seems odd not to ask them if——'

'You're right,' he broke in. 'I'm sorry, of course we'll invite them.'

But, though he'd agreed without an argument, Dita felt sure he didn't want them there, and wondered why not.

There was a short, rather strained silence before he remarked abruptly, 'You look tired.'

'I am,' she admitted, starting to feel the effects of what had been a disturbing, not to say traumatic evening.

With a brittle flash of humour, he said, 'In that case, I'll walk you home.'

Longing for some warmth, some small sign of affection, she had hoped he would take her in his arms, hold her close and ask her to stay. But, despite his earlier remark about sating himself with her, he was acting as if he no longer even *wanted* her, she thought in confusion, as he escorted her to the lift with distant politeness.

This feeling of being unwanted, discarded, was compounded when, with just a cool 'Goodnight,' he left her at her door.

Though more than ready for bed, when she finally slid between the sheets Dita found herself unable to sleep. So much had happened. So much of it disturbing in the extreme.

When she had walked into Rider's apartment and caught him unawares, she could have sworn he was suffering because he thought she'd gone. Yet his subsequent behaviour didn't bear that out.

She had hoped, prayed that what he felt for her was more than just desire. His insistence—even after her confession—that having her for his wife was of paramount importance had sent hope winging sky-high, only to have it plummet to earth like Icarus, when all he would admit to was an obsession.

An obsession... The thought both upset and frightened her. But though he might not love her *she* loved *him*, and, having burnt her boats well and truly, there was no going back. So she must go ahead and marry him, try to put the guilt over Stephen and the accident behind her, and make Rider so happy that he wouldn't want to look at another woman.

She sighed, hardly able to believe that in a few short weeks she would be his wife. Images of him filled her mind. As he was now, hard, stern-faced, obsessed. As he'd been when they'd first met, easy, smiling, carefree.

Though refusing to acknowledge it, to admit it even to herself, she had loved him from that very first moment. And, according to him, he'd felt the same about her. She recalled his apparent sincerity when he'd said, 'I knew I wanted to marry you the first day I walked into Tim Ryan's office and saw you sitting behind that desk so cool and prim'...

So what had happened? What had gone wrong?

Showing quiet determination and patience, he had courted her—it was an old-fashioned word but appropriate—and taken endless trouble to overcome her doubts and prove to her that she could fit into his world. But why—when all the time he was lying to her, deceiving her, having an affair with Julie Dawn—had he bothered?

As though by reliving it she could finally understand, get it into perspective, she deliberately let her thoughts travel back to their very first meeting.

He had strolled into her office one lovely June day, a man of about twenty-eight, with wide-set grey eyes in a face too strong and hard-bitten to be termed truly handsome; a sophisticated man who wore an air of power and authority as easily as he wore his hand-tailored suit...

CHAPTER SIX

'MISS P. GREER.' Palms spread flat on her desk, the newcomer read the plastic identity strip which Tim Ryan liked all his staff to display. 'P. Greer?' He made it a question.

'Yes,' she replied unhelpfully. He was too good-looking—with a hawk-like, Aztec kind of bone-structure—too sure of himself. 'Have you an appointment?' she added politely.

He shook his fair head. 'Not exactly. What does the P stand for?' When she didn't answer he began to guess. 'Paula? Pamela? Patricia...?' Having reeled off a string of names without getting any response, he paused to complain with mock-severity, 'If you won't tell me, how can I get to know you any better?'

With no desire to be known better, she asked distantly, 'Is it Mr Ryan you wish to see?'

'I *did*, but I think I've changed my mind... Having discovered——'

'If you'd like to give me your name,' she broke in smoothly, 'I'll find out if he's available.'

'Oh, he'll be available,' the man said confidently.

Before she could ask him again for his name, the door of the inner office opened and her boss appeared.

At the sight of his visitor he stopped dead. 'Why, Mr Barron!' he exclaimed. 'I hadn't expected a personal visit.' He sounded so effusive that Dita suddenly appreciated that this blond giant was no ordinary caller.

Barron...she pondered as Tim Ryan ushered his visitor into the inner sanctum. Of course, *Rider Barron*, from

the investment banking firm! No wonder his sudden un-
heralded appearance had thrown her boss.

It was less than fifteen minutes before the door opened
and the two men emerged, talking amiably. They shook
hands, and Rider Barron gave Dita an ironic little salute
before leaving.

She watched him walk out of her life with a little sigh
of what she told herself was relief, even if it felt uncomfortably like regret.

Next day he blew in again fresh as a prairie wind, and,
leaning casually on her desk, gazed down at her. Taking
in the glossy black hair that curled around her delicate
oval face, the green eyes that looked back at him so
steadily from beneath winged brows, the fine, straight
nose, the warm curve of her mouth, he murmured, 'So
I wasn't mistaken.'

His smile hit her like a sock on the jaw and sent her
reeling.

Softly, he went on, 'P. Greer, you are the most hauntingly beautiful thing I've ever seen. But it's the character
in your face that makes it so fascinating and
unforgettable.'

Thrown by his words and the lick of flame in his grey
eyes, she said jerkily, 'I'll let Mr Ryan know you're here.'
But as she stretched out a hand to flick the intercom
switch he took possession of it.

His thumb lightly brushing the smooth, inner skin of
her wrist, he said calmly, 'It wasn't Ryan I came to see.
Have dinner with me tonight?'

'No, thank you, Mr Barron.' She spoke steadily now,
though her heart was racing with suffocating speed.

'Call me Rider,' he invited. Then, 'Tomorrow night?'
Pulling her hand free, she shook her head.

Raising a level brow several shades darker than his thick blond hair, he asked, 'Is there a steady boyfriend? A live-in lover, perhaps?'

'No, there is not.'

'That was very positive. Do I detect a girl with good old-fashioned principles?'

Catching a hint of mockery, she answered briskly, 'Just a female who prefers her own company to that of the predatory, business-suited male.'

His grey eyes danced so beguilingly that she had a job to keep her mouth prim.

Watching her, he suggested, 'Couldn't you relax and smile?'

'I will when you've gone,' she promised.

Undisturbed, he returned the attack. 'If I give you my word to be a model of rectitude, will you come out with me?'

'No,' she reiterated flatly.

'Why not?' he demanded.

She was saved from having to answer by the inner door opening and Tim Ryan appearing. Dita breathed a sigh of relief as her tormentor was greeted and led away. Over his shoulder he gave her a wryly comical glance.

Once the door was closed she chuckled to herself. At least he had the saving grace of humour... But he was a wealthy man from a world of bright lights and lax morals, definitely not the kind of man she could ever allow herself to get involved with...

Over the following weeks she stuck to her resolve, though he returned time and again. Subconsciously she began to look forward to his daily visits, to feel a surge of excitement, and something else she preferred not to analyse, when he appeared at her desk.

Then one Monday he didn't come. When that day stretched to four, she knew he'd given up. She told herself she was relieved. But his absence had torn a gaping hole in the structure of her life, through which a cold wind blew.

On Friday afternoon she was standing by her shelves reaching for a reference book when his clear, low-pitched voice murmured in her ear, 'Missed me?'

Hardly able to conceal the unbidden flood of joy that washed over her, she said repressively, 'The last few days have been very peaceful.'

'Don't you mean dull?'

Had he stayed away deliberately? Was trying to make her miss him part of his strategy? If so, it had worked, she admitted ruefully. If she'd been a dog her tail would have been wagging.

His white grin flashed and she knew he'd read her mind.

He was standing by her side and his closeness made her hot and bothered. Hurriedly she moved to her chair and sat down, feeling less vulnerable with the desk between them.

'I've been in L.A.,' he informed her cheerfully. 'Just got back.' He came to sit on the edge of her desk. 'Have dinner with me tonight to celebrate my return?'

Refusing to look at him, she shook her head.

He put a finger beneath her chin and lifted her face. 'Why not? You know you want to.'

Jerking away from his touch, she denied, 'I *don't* want to go out with you.' Then, in desperation, 'If you don't leave me alone, I'll report you for sexual harassment.'

'You're behaving like an outraged virgin,' he told her.

His obvious amusement was the last straw. 'All right,' she turned on him furiously, 'perhaps that's what I am. Now laugh!'

'I've no intention of laughing,' he assured her, straight-faced. 'I just don't see the need to be outraged. I'm only suggesting we have a meal together; I'm not asking you to move in with me.'

His gentle rebuke made her feel foolish, as perhaps he'd intended. He touched her hot cheek with a cool finger. 'Where do you live?'

Like someone under hypnosis, she told him.

'I'll pick you up this evening around seven-thirty.' At the door he turned to say, 'By the way, I still don't know your name. Ryan always refers to you very properly as Miss Greer, and I haven't had the nerve to ask him.'

She smiled at the thought of this man being short of nerve, and, suddenly feeling glowingly alive and light-hearted, admitted, 'My name's Perdita.'

He surprised her by commenting, 'Somehow it suits you.'

Embarrassed by the way he was gazing at her, his look almost a caress, she added hastily, 'But I always get called Dita.'

Shaking his blond head, he assured her, 'Not by me, you won't. See you tonight, Perdita.'

After their first date her resistance melted like an icicle in the Nevada sun, and he took her out regularly. Always he escorted her home to her apartment building, which was old and shabby but had a superb view across the Upper Bay to the Statue of Liberty, and left her at her door with a platonic, 'Goodnight, sleep well.' Yet each time he looked at her there was a tiny lick of flame which told her how badly he wanted her.

It was like watching a lit fuse travelling towards a keg of dynamite. But she couldn't find the strength to end their relationship.

One warm late-summer evening, having got her home early, he suggested a walk in Battery Park. Talking idly, they strolled through the blue dusk. The balmy air carried a salt tang from the Bay, and in the background the Hudson river made a shining floor.

Suddenly Rider stopped and turned towards her. As she gazed at him uncertainly he bent and, without holding her in any way, touched his mouth to hers.

Taken by surprise, she responded with all the passionate warmth, the sweet hunger that lay hidden beneath her cool self-possession.

He made a funny little sound and, taking her into his arms, deepened the kiss until her head was spinning madly and her body was on fire, crazy for his touch, his possession.

Pop music blaring from a transistor radio brought an abrupt return to sanity. She pulled herself free, her heart pounding as if she'd just run a race.

'I ought to be getting home.' Her voice sounded as shaken as she felt. 'It's work tomorrow.'

At her door he drew her into his arms and bent to kiss her. Somehow she kept her lips tightly closed.

He stopped kissing her and gave an elaborate sigh. She thought she'd won, but he forced her chin up so that the lamplight fell on her face. 'Oh, no, Perdita,' he said softly, 'I've played a waiting game long enough. I won't allow you to retreat behind those barricades again.'

All at once he gave her ear a sharp nip, and when her lips parted on a startled gasp he swooped and claimed her mouth, kissing her deeply, urgently, until her senses swam and she was forced to cling to him.

When he finally freed her lips, he said evenly, 'Tomorrow evening I'll pick you up straight from work. I thought we'd go to...'

But she was already shaking her head, panicky words spilling out. 'I won't be coming. I don't want to see you again...'

'Liar.'

'Please, Rider,' she begged unsteadily, 'leave me alone. We have totally different lifestyles. I'm not your kind of woman.'

'Oh?' he said, quietly dangerous. 'And what is my kind of woman?'

'You know quite well. Someone who has wealth and position, who belongs in your social class.'

'I don't need a woman to have wealth or position, I've enough for both those commodities. And as far as I'm concerned you have more "class" than any other female I've ever met.'

She shook her head despairingly. 'I could never fit into your world.'

His hands fastened on to her shoulders, his fingers biting in. 'How do you know unless you try?' Masterfully, he added, 'Now no more nonsense, do you hear? Or I'll be tempted to take you over my knee and beat some sense into you.'

Drawing her back into his arms, he kissed her with great thoroughness. Then, his lips muffled against her silky hair, he said softly, 'From now on things are going to be very different.'

Until then *she* had been setting the terms of their relationship. After that night, *he* was. There were no more quiet dinners in out-of-the-way restaurants, no careful keeping apart of their two worlds.

Encased in happiness, beautiful and fragile as rainbow glass, she lived from day to day, refusing to think about the future or how things might end.

Both the Barrons, father and son, shared playboy images, and for years the wealthy, somewhat flamboyant pair had been meat and drink to the gossip columnists.

As soon as Rider started to take Dita to well-known night spots and introduce her to his friends, the Press began to speculate about this unknown woman in his life. They discovered she was an ordinary working girl who lived downtown in a seedy apartment building, and for a while had a field day. When that palled they dug up what little there was to know about her past, but it was so blameless that they dubbed her 'The Mystery Woman'.

Then, for several weeks, apparently unable to rake up anything that was 'news' the media gave them a rest.

When Dita expressed relief, Rider said cynically, 'Make the most of it. It won't last.'

On the following Saturday morning he was proved right, as Dita discovered when she glanced through the paper while she drank her breakfast coffee.

The news had just broken that Julie Dawn, the dancer who played glamorous Tamara Darling in the Broadway musical *Long Live Tomorrow*, was pulling out of the show.

When asked why she was leaving, Ms Dawn told our correspondent, 'For the most wonderful reason in the world. I'm going to have a baby'.

The beautiful redhead, who gives her age as thirty-four, admitted that the pregnancy hadn't been planned, and the producers of *Long Live Tomorrow* were furious. Understandably, as the show already shows signs of being a flop.

When asked the identity of the baby's father, the star turned coy and refused to say, but she did let slip that he belonged to a wealthy banking family.

Rumour has it that, despite his apparent attachment to working girl Perdita Greer, Rider Barron is the secret man in Ms Dawn's life...

Perdita threw the paper aside in disgust. When it came to maligning the rich and famous, did the gutter Press never give up?

When, some three quarters of an hour later, Rider rang the bell of her small apartment, she was still simmering with rage. Quick to pick up her mood, he asked, 'Is something the matter?'

'No, not really.' She tried to sound airy, dismissive.

Cupping her chin, he lifted her face so that he could look deep into her green eyes. 'Come on, out with it. What's bothering you?'

Sighing, she told him.

Stroking his thumb along the clean line of her jaw, he said decidedly, 'Don't let yourself be upset by such garbage. *You* are the only woman in my life.' He stooped and kissed her in a way that caused her toes to curl and sent shivers of pleasure up and down her spine.

It was a glorious autumn day, and, looking forward to spending it in the open air, she'd donned a cotton dress and sandals, but instead of his customary casually elegant weekend clothes Rider was wearing a formal suit.

Raising a dark brow, she asked, 'Going somewhere special?'

'We're joining my parents for lunch at the Waldorf,' he told her easily. 'They're on the political circuit, helping with the party campaigning.

'I know this isn't the ideal way to meet them, but they have a very tight schedule and they'll be on their travels again in a few days.' Watching her perturbation, he added, 'If politics bore you we can slip away before the speeches start.'

'It's not that,' she managed. 'I . . . I don't know what to wear. Oh, *why* didn't you give me some warning?'

'Do you take me for a fool, Perdita?'

He was quite right. If he hadn't sprung it on her she would have found a way to wriggle out of going.

Glancing at his slim Cartier watch, he said briskly, 'You've half an hour to get ready.' Then, dropping a light kiss on her nose, he added, his voice warmer and deeper, 'Don't worry, you'll more than hold your own whatever you wear.'

On an earlier occasion when she'd tried to get out of going to a society party by protesting—truthfully—that she hadn't a suitable dress, he'd offered to take her to Saks on Fifth Avenue and buy her a whole new wardrobe.

She'd turned on him furiously. 'Just what kind of woman do you think I am?'

'I know what kind of woman you are,' he'd replied immediately. 'Proud, independent, obstinate, infuriating, and *beautiful*. So beautiful it doesn't matter a toss what you wear. If you went in an old sack all the women would still envy you and all the men would envy me.'

Now she decided on an uncrushable suit in subtle autumn shades and, with ten minutes to spare, presented herself for Rider's inspection.

'Perfect.' He gave her a smile that made her heart do a back somersault, and followed her out.

'Are you interested in politics?' she enquired as they drove uptown.

'Not especially,' he answered. 'Though as well as my father I've a stepbrother and two cousins all attempting to climb the political ladder.'

Idly she asked, 'Will they succeed, do you think?'

'My father might. To make the top a politician needs to be both ruthless and strong; weaker people only make the rungs.'

Dita had noticed that whenever he mentioned his father Rider's voice had a hard, unforgiving edge to it.

But, his tone softening, he was going on, 'You'll like Kate, my stepmother. She's a really nice person.'

'How long have they been married?'

'About seven years. Kate was a widow with a grown-up son when they met.'

'Is your mother still alive?'

'No, she died while I was at university.'

Catching an underlying bitterness, Dita asked no further questions, and they relapsed into silence until they reached Park Avenue.

She had never been inside the Waldorf Astoria before, and she glanced around the art deco lobby with interest before Rider took her arm and steered her towards a couple who were approaching.

The woman was dark and petite, with forget-me-not blue eyes and a friendly, vivacious face. The man was tall and well-built, eyes grey, thick hair an attractive silver-gilt. His face was heavier than his son's, his mouth fuller and betraying a hint of self-indulgence.

The two men shook hands formally, then Rider stooped to kiss the woman's cheek. 'Nice to see you. It's been a long time.'

'Too long,' she replied in a clear, musical voice. Then, holding out her hand to Dita, she went on, 'We won't stand on ceremony. I'm Kate, you must be Perdita. Rider told me all about you over the phone . . .'

Any awkwardness Dita might have felt was washed away by the flow of words. She smiled at Kate grate-fully, sensing that the other woman was trying hard to put her at her ease.

'And this is my husband, another Rider, though I always call him Dan, short for Daniel, his middle name.'

It was obvious where Rider got his blazing charm, Dita thought as she shook hands with his father and received a stunning smile. But while Rider's charm seemed natural, spontaneous, the older man's had a polished, practised feel to it. Perhaps because he was a politician? she concluded.

He offered her his arm, leaving his wife and son to follow behind. 'I understand you used to live in Washington, DC? Hopefully we'll be moving there before too long...'

The food was excellent, the conversation free and wide-ranging, and lunch passed quickly with none of the awkwardness Dita had feared.

They had finished coffee and were on the point of leaving when Kate suddenly exclaimed, 'I almost forgot, we're giving a party on Thursday! Small, but glittering, I hope. All the V.I.P.s, the upper echelon...'

'I thought you were on the point of closing your house down?' Rider remarked.

'We've done it. Staff gone, dust sheets in place. We're staying here until we hit the road... Now about this party—you will come, won't you?' Her smiling glance included Dita. 'Eight o'clock, in our suite.'

'Your timing's abysmal,' Rider complained. 'I should be on a plane bound for San Francisco that evening, but I guess I can catch an early flight next morning. Yes, we'll be there,' he confirmed, adding casually, 'Won't we, honey?'

'I... Well, I don't know if...' Startled by the 'honey' and unable, on the spur of the moment, to think of any excuse for not going, Dita floundered and stopped.

Rider flicked her cheek with a lean finger. Though it must have looked like a light caress, it might have been the warning flick of a rapier. 'I'm sure it's nothing we can't sort out.'

'Good,' Kate said cheerfully. 'See you then.'

At soon as they were outside on the sunny pavement, Dita protested, 'Why did you say we'd go?'

He smiled tigerishly, gleaming grey eyes narrowed against the glare. 'Because it's the final hurdle. Once you're over that you'll have nothing left to fear.'

But she was far from reassured. The following Tuesday afternoon she asked for a couple of hours off work and went shopping.

Light as a breeze, the simply styled chiffon dress in sea colours of cobalt, jade and gold took her eye at once. She tried it on and, deciding it had been made for her, splurged with her credit card.

Even knowing she would look her best failed to relieve her anxieties, however, and by the time Thursday came she felt nervous and gloomy.

Her dismal mood wasn't helped by the morning paper. It carried a photograph of Rider, looking furious, with the caption 'Wealthy banker denies paternity.'

Underneath, the report continued.

On Wall Street yesterday, we talked to Rider Barron, who angrily repudiated repeated rumours that he is the father of Julie Dawn's expected baby.

'It's utter rubbish,' he declared. 'I've never even met the woman.'

Dita sighed. He must be fed up with being hounded.

When Rider called to pick her up at seven-thirty that evening she was ready and waiting, her nails polished, her make-up flawless, her black silky curls stylishly upswept with only the odd tendril loose around her face.

His appreciative glance told her more eloquently than words that she looked good.

During the drive uptown, Rider was talkative and smiling, clearly looking forward to the evening. 'Though it's rather a pity to have to be at the airport so early tomorrow,' he remarked.

'Is it likely to be a late party?' Dita asked.

'Kate's "do"s often go on until the small hours of the morning, though I wasn't thinking of staying much after twelve...If you like we can leave earlier.'

Shaking her head, she said, 'I'll be happy to stay until midnight.'

He slanted her a mocking glance. 'How exciting! I never envisaged having my very own Cinderella.'

She wrinkled her nose at him. 'Any more than I envisaged having my very own Rockefeller.'

As they drew up at a red light he reached for her hand and gave it a squeeze. Then he turned his head and, his clear grey eyes smiling into hers, said softly, 'I love you.'

It was what she'd longed to hear. She arrived at the party incandescent with joy, glowing with happiness, and without a jewel to her name easily outshone every other woman there.

Enjoying herself, she hadn't noticed the time flying, and was surprised when Rider took her empty champagne glass from her and murmured, 'Come on, Cinderella, it's almost midnight and your coach is waiting.'

She smiled at him. 'Are you sure I'll make it? I don't want my finery to turn to rags before it's even paid for.'

'I'm sure of one thing—there'd be an almighty rush to pick up the glass slipper. Your brief whirl through the power and politics scene has been something of a *tour de force.*'

He was exaggerating, of course. But still she was thrilled by his words. Maybe it wouldn't be too difficult to fit into his world, after all.

When they said their goodbyes and slipped away, the party was still in full swing.

It must have been obvious that *she* had been in no hurry to leave, and, knowing him well enough to be certain that tomorrow's early start hadn't been the cause, Dita wondered why Rider had cut the evening short. Her question was soon answered.

Once behind the wheel of his sleek car he lifted her hand to his lips and kissed the palm, then instead of turning downtown he drove towards Fifth Avenue and his penthouse.

Her silence was a tacit acceptance of the fact.

In the comfortable living-room he slipped the light wrap from her shoulders and touched his lips to the warmth of her nape. She shivered deliciously and when he turned her into his arms lifted her mouth for his kiss with complete trust.

Somehow the miracle had happened and he loved her. He had said so, and she never doubted it for a moment. It was everything she could have hoped for, and more.

Taking her hand, he led her into his bedroom and, closing the door behind them, kissed her with a sweet, passionate hunger. When he lifted his head she was breathless, the convulsive clutch of desire deep inside her.

He undressed her without haste, savouring every moment. No gauche fumbling boy, this, but a man who knew just where to touch and stroke, how to build and prolong pleasure as his hands explored with sensuous appreciation.

He lifted her on to the bed and she watched with a kind of breathless fascination while he stripped off his own clothes. Again he moved unhurriedly, giving her time to appreciate his smooth, golden skin, the rippling muscles of his broad chest and shoulders, his flat stomach and lean hips, the long, powerful legs with their fuzz of golden hair.

Oh, but he was beautiful. An Adonis. Except that he was no mere youth. He was mature, virile. All man.

He laughed, a husky chuckle that said plainer than words how much her guileless appraisal was arousing him. Realising she was staring as though mesmerised, she blushed hotly and lifted her eyes.

Stretching out beside her, he leaned over her and began to kiss her again, the tip of his tongue delicately touching and stimulating. Then, while his hands made their own exploration, his mouth began to rove over her breasts, enjoying the pale, silky skin, the firm, dusky pink nipples.

His erotic suckling, combined with the movement of his fingers, made her gasp and catch at his wrist.

'Don't you like that?' he asked softly.

'Oh, *yes*,' she breathed. 'But I . . . I want *you* to enjoy it too.'

Rider smiled, his grey eyes full of a quizzical tenderness. 'My precious love, you really are an innocent, aren't you?'

'I suppose I'm very dull and——'

'Never dull,' he interrupted swiftly. 'Different. In fact I rather suspect you're unique.'

'You must be very experienced,' she said a shade wistfully, trying not to dwell on how so much experience had been gained.

'I haven't lived like a monk,' he admitted, 'but neither have I been promiscuous, as the gutter Press would have their readers believe.'

'How on earth do they come by all those stories?' she wondered aloud.

He answered a shade bitterly, 'They're truly creative. What they can't find out they make up.'

'Does it worry you?'

'Not as a rule. Mainly I take their libellous rubbish in my stride. But why are we wasting time talking?'

'It's my fault,' she admitted. 'I put you off. I'm a fool.'

He shook his head. 'You are a delight.'

Their loving was sweet and passionate, tender and caring, wild and exhilarating, and she never wanted it to end.

When it finally did, she hoped to lie awake and savour it but, held against his heart, she slipped all too quickly into sleep.

Next morning she awoke to instant and complete remembrance. Happiness filling her, she turned her head to smile at Rider, only to find she was alone in the king-sized divan.

A glance at the bedside clock told her it was almost nine. She sat up abruptly. He must have left for the airport hours ago.

When she discovered the folded piece of paper on the bedside cabinet, some of her despondency at finding him already gone vanished, and she snatched it up, her spirits rising. He'd written the note in a strong black scrawl.

Darling, I've always disliked parting from you, even for a short while, and after last night it's even harder.

I didn't *intend* it to happen. I should have waited until I got back instead of rushing things. But I can't be sorry.

The conference, a weekend one, begins this evening. So I should be free to fly home Monday. It can't be soon enough. When I get back we'll talk about the future and make plans.

I love you. Rider

PS. Because of your finery, you'll need to take a taxi home.

Only then did she notice the dollar bills lying there. She blessed his thoughtfulness. And he was right;

though it would take up valuable time, she couldn't go into the office dressed as she was.

Despite Tim Ryan's annoyance at her being late, the day was one of the happiest of her life and she got home from work that evening with a smile on her lips.

As she fitted her key into the lock, a voice said, 'Hi, hope you don't mind me asking, but do you happen to have a phone?'

It was the pleasant, red-headed man who lived in the apartment above her own. They'd exchanged a few words from time to time when they passed on the stairs, and she'd thought idly that he was nice. But she knew little about him except that his name was Stephen West, he was a chef, and, like herself, a relative newcomer to New York, having been raised in Georgia.

'I'm sorry, I don't,' she said in answer to his question.

'Oh, well, I guess I'll go and have a pizza at Joe's and ring from there.'

Dita had turned away when he added diffidently, 'I don't suppose you'd care to join me? For a pizza, I mean. They're the best in town.' As she hesitated, he added, 'You look happy, and I could do with some cheering up.'

She had no plans for the evening, and Stephen sounded so forlorn that her soft heart was touched. Making up her mind, she said, 'Yes, I'd like that.'

He smiled, his bright blue eyes open and guileless. 'Wonderful!'

'Why do you need cheering up?' she asked, as they made their way through the busy streets to Joe's.

'During the last couple of weeks I've lost both my girlfriend and my job.' He grinned crookedly. 'And the rent's due in a few days...'

'If you need a loan...?' Dita began.

'You're a doll,' he said gratefully, 'but I've finally decided the best thing I can do is go back to Georgia for a spell and stay with Ma. She's had a slight stroke, and her doctor thinks it would be better if she wasn't living alone, at least until she's fully recovered.

'Her house is just outside Atlanta. I should be able to get a job there, and when I've managed to save enough, and she's feeling better again, I'll have another shot at the real bright lights...'

Sitting over a Margherite and a bottle of cheap red wine, they talked like old friends, and it was eleven-thirty when finally he escorted her to her door.

His blue eyes hopeful, he asked, 'I don't suppose you'll invite me in for coffee?'

Smiling, so that it wouldn't seem like a snub, she answered, 'You don't suppose right.'

'Is there someone special in your life?'

'Very special,' she replied softly, her face aglow.

He sighed. 'Ah, well, you're not only beautiful, but kind and sweet too, so that's only to be expected. Thanks for your company, honeychild. If you're at home in the morning I'll give you a knock to say goodbye.'

As soon as he'd gone, Stephen faded from her mind and she went to sleep to dream of Rider. Her first thought when she awoke was that there was only two days to go before she saw him again.

But, as she sat down to her coffee and toast and opened the paper, his face, wearing an angry, thin-lipped expression, looked up at her from the front page. The caption beneath read, 'Banker finally admits paternity! Full story, by Nick Marsh, our special correspondent, page seven.'

Turning to page seven, with hands that shook, Dita read on.

I finally caught up with Rider Barron yesterday morning at LaGuardia as he was about to board a plane for San Francisco.

Faced with irrefutable evidence—the name of the motel where the couple had frequently stayed, and several signed bills—Barron admitted that he was Julie Dawn's lover.

Asked if he was planning to marry Ms Dawn, the banker refused to make any further comment except to say that if the 'digging for dirt', as he put it, didn't stop, he would—and I quote—'break my bloody neck.'

Dita stared at the damning paragraphs until the words danced before her eyes, then, dropping the paper, she sat gazing blindly into space...

Her face buried in the pillow, Dita choked on a sob. Even after all this time the memory was unbearable, and reliving the past had served no useful purpose. She was no nearer understanding.

Perhaps she cried in her sleep, because the next morning her pillow was still damp.

CHAPTER SEVEN

SOME five weeks later, all the formalities having been attended to, Dita and Rider were married by the spare and laconic Reverend Jesse Lee James at noon on the chosen day.

While the bride looked a picture in an ivory cashmere dress and jacket, a delicate pink orchid pinned to the lapel, the groom was devastatingly handsome in pearl-grey with a cream carnation in his buttonhole.

They had decided against New York City as a venue in case the Press got wind of it, and the simple ceremony took place in the small, picturesque Catskill village of Owlport, not far from Rider's Keep.

The little wooden chapel was cold, and bare, and starkly beautiful, with white plaster walls, clear diamond-leaded windows and a vaulted roof.

Mrs Merriton was there, arrayed in a flower-decked hat of such startling unbecomingness that Dita's composure was threatened even before Rider suggested, *sotto voce*, that it must have looked better on the horse.

Apart from the witnesses—an old couple who lived in the clapboard house adjoining the chapel—the only other people present were Rider's father and stepmother.

They arrived just before the ceremony began, and, though both of them hugged the bride and said repeatedly how delighted they were, the atmosphere was strained.

Afterwards, Mrs Merriton having insisted on returning to Rider's Keep, they joined the newly-weds to

walk the short distance to the sprawling, timber-built Owl
Inn for lunch.

It was a cold, crisp December day, with flurries of
snow too light to settle. On leaving the shelter of the
chapel's wooden porch a handful of fine snowflakes
swirled and settled on the bridal party like confetti,
spangling Dita's crown of dark hair and melting on her
long, thick lashes.

Though unpretentious, the meal, served in the almost
deserted dining-room in front of a crackling log fire,
was very good, but even the vintage champagne which
accompanied it failed to loosen tongues or lessen the
tension to any great degree.

'Your invitation came right out of the blue,' Kate observed after an awkward pause. 'And we were so *pleased*.
We had no idea that you and Rider had got together
again.' Flushing a little, she went on, 'Now we live per-
manently in Washington, DC and only make flying visits
to New York, it isn't as easy to keep in touch.'

But Dita felt sure there was a lot more to it than that,
and wondered why the older woman should be so obviously embarrassed and ill at ease.

As, once again, the silence threatened to become op-
pressive, Kate asked brightly, 'Are you having a
honeymoon?'

'Yes,' Dita answered reluctantly.

'Where are you heading for? Or is it a secret?'

Making an effort to smile, Dita said, 'It's a secret.
Even I don't know where we're going.'

'How thrilling!' Kate exclaimed. 'You must be terribly excited.'

Doing her best to fit the role assigned to her, Dita
said, 'Yes, I am,' but was unhappily aware that her voice
lacked conviction. Looking up, she flushed as she met
Rider's sardonic gaze, and, desperate to change the

subject, asked, 'Do you prefer Washington to New York?'

Talking about the capital tided them over until they'd finished coffee. Then, while the two men waited in a lobby which was redolent of pine cones and resin, and talked politics in a desultory fashion, the women went to freshen up.

Kate, looking elegant in a coral-coloured suit, patted a stray dark hair into place and powdered her nose unnecessarily before blurting out, 'It was nice of you to invite us. I can't tell you what a relief it is to know that you and Rider are finally married. I was so afraid that Julie Dawn——' Kate broke off, biting her lip.

After a second she went on, 'He was like a man possessed after you disappeared, and I felt so *guilty*... Unless you've experienced guilt you can't know how it keeps you awake at night, eats into your soul like acid...'

Dita knew only too well. Though she hadn't the faintest idea why the older woman should feel guilty.

'I suppose Rider's told you everything,' Kate was rushing on, 'but one day soon I'd like to have a long heart-to-heart, really clear the air...'

Before Dita could frame any questions, Kate caught sight of the old-fashioned wall-clock and exclaimed in horror, 'Good lord, it's almost two-thirty!'

Turning, she began to hurry back to the lobby, talking as she went. 'If we don't set off straight away we won't get to the airport in time to catch our plane. Dan and I are spending Christmas in Hawaii with some friends, so I'm looking forward to a spot of sunshine...'

Farewells made, they went outside to where both cars were waiting and the chill air carried the scent of woodsmoke. As Kate took her place in the Mercedes, Dita said swiftly, 'Enjoy your holiday, and when you get back give me a ring so we can have that heart-to-heart you mentioned.'

Though she wasn't looking at Rider she was aware that he stiffened and glanced at her sharply. She tried to tell herself that the sudden shiver which ran through her was caused by the cold wind driving another light snow-flurry.

When the older couple had driven off, he settled Dita in her seat and got behind the wheel of the silver-grey BMW without a word.

As they left the Inn, with its chalet-type roof and overhanging veranda, and took the winding road up into the mountains, she glanced at his hard profile and wondered what was going through his mind.

Well, there was only one way to find out. Giving herself no time to reconsider, she asked, 'Rider...what are you thinking?'

He gave her a mocking glance. 'Do you subscribe to the notion that a wife's prerogative extends to knowing her husband's thoughts?'

She persevered. 'Are you sorry you went through with this marriage?'

'It's a bit late now for regrets.' Shrugging, he echoed the words she'd once used. 'Are *you* having second thoughts?'

She hadn't been until Kate's mention of Julie Dawn had unsettled her, making her wonder if this uneasy union would ever work.

Now, in the face of Rider's apparent indifference, she felt even more confused and doubtful. Unwilling to admit it, she said briskly, 'No, I prefer to pay my debts,' and registered his anger with some satisfaction.

Since the night they'd made love in his penthouse, he'd neither touched nor kissed her. Over the following days they'd met to talk and make plans for the wedding, but

on each occasion he'd treated her with an aloof politeness that kept her at a distance.

November and December had been comparatively mild
with hardly any snowfall, so the ground was dry and
clear. But, as they climbed higher through forested slopes
which had once been densely covered with hemlock, snow
began to fall in earnest, big soft flakes that drifted against
the windscreen like curly feathers, making it necessary
for Rider to flick on the wipers.

It looked like being a white Christmas.

When she'd shopped for a small trousseau, and everything else had been duly settled, he'd brought up the
topic of their honeymoon again. 'As neither of us has
had a holiday this year, I suggest we take at least a couple
of weeks... Unless, of course, you're dead set against
it?'

This time Dita had done her best to appear enthusi-
astic. 'No... no, I'd like to go. But could we find some-
place... different, do you think? Somewhere with not
too many people?' Memories she still couldn't cope with
crowding in on her, she'd added desperately, 'Honeymoons can be so *public*.'

He'd studied her thoughtfully. 'The world's your
oyster. If you tell me what you have in mind, I'll arrange
it.'

Wanting only to stay at home, she'd hesitated, biting
her lip. 'I don't really have anything in mind...'

Holding on to the coat-tails of his patience, he'd asked,
'Surely there's somewhere you fancy, Perdita? The
Seychelles? Idaho? New Mexico? None of those are over-
populated.'

Feeling sick panic rising inside her, she'd muttered,
'Oh, anywhere you like. I don't really mind
where we go.'

His face settling into a frigid mask, Rider had said,
'Then perhaps I should surprise you.'

Apart from warning her to pack some warm clothes,
he'd said nothing further, and the subject hadn't been
mentioned again until lunchtime today.

Now, with no idea where they were going except that
they appeared to be heading into the Catskills, Dita broke
the lengthening silence to ask, 'Have we far to travel?'
and was dismayed by how wavery her voice sounded.

Without glancing at her, he answered levelly, 'We
should be there before dark.'

With pristine valleys, clear streams, and beautiful
scenery, the Catskills were, at all seasons, a Mecca for
holiday-makers and tourists, and boasted a variety and
plentiful supply of resorts and accommodation.

Expecting their destination to be one of the quieter
lakeside hotels, Dita was startled when, just as dusk had
started to spread grey, gauzy nets to catch the drifting
white flakes, they turned off the hill road and bumped
down a narrow dirt track. After a hundred metres or so,
the track widened out into a clearing and they drew to
a halt in front of an old log cabin with a tumbledown
lean-to attached to one side.

Without a word Rider got out and, having helped her
from the car, produced a large key and crossed the
sagging wooden porch to unlock the door.

As she hesitated on the threshold, with an ironic smile
curving his lips he swung her up into his arms and carried
her into the gloom, setting her on her feet in the middle
of the bare floor.

She glanced around the large room, nonplussed. A
minimum of rough furniture and a few hand-pegged rugs
was all it contained, while the kitchen facilities appeared
to consist of several cupboards, a food store, and a deep
porcelain sink with a hand-pump. The air was as cold

inside as out, but her heart lifted to see huge piles of logs and kindling stacked each side of the big black, open-fronted range.

'What do you think of our honeymoon house, Perdita?' There was a gleam in Rider's grey eyes which convinced her that, perhaps as a kind of retribution, he'd *intended* to startle and disconcert her.

Determined not to let him see he'd done both, she made her smile serene, her voice cheerful, as she answered, 'It's certainly different. And I can't imagine we'll suffer from lack of privacy.'

'So you like it?' he goaded.

'Love it.' She repressed a shiver. 'As soon as we've got a fire going it'll seem like home.' Realising with a little thrill of triumph that she'd succeeded in turning the tables, she added sweetly, 'If it keeps on snowing it may *be* home until next spring.'

Hiding his chagrin well, he disagreed, 'I don't think it'll come to that. There are snow-chains in the trunk and I understand the cabin is equipped with skis.'

'Is it equipped with food?' A little tartness crept in. 'Or do we have to hunt our own?'

'We have four cartons of supplies, not to mention a selection of wine and spirits and several bottles of champagne.' He gave her a glinting look. 'In case boredom sets in there's a big box of books and games; we've also got a couple of torches, a good supply of matches, and plenty of oil for the lamps.'

Resisting the temptation to ask him if he'd been reading *Boys' Own*, she exclaimed in mock-admiration, 'My, but you *have* got everything under control!'

'I think so.' As well as a decided challenge, those three innocuous words held a silky menace that made little prickles of nameless apprehension run down Dita's spine and told her he was undoubtedly master of the situation once more.

While he went to bring in their luggage and the various boxes, she selected some dry kindling and, having discovered a tin of matches on a shelf, set about lighting a fire.

With scant regard for her wedding finery she went down on her hands and knees to blow the flickering flame into a blaze. When the split logs crackled and flared, she brushed a tendril of hair away from her cheek and sat back on her haunches to admire her handiwork.

'You've done a good job there,' Rider remarked.

'Do you know that's the first time I've ever had to cope with an old-fashioned range?' she announced proudly.

'Then you won't have cooked on one?' he asked blandly.

Hoping he was joking, she assured him, 'I've always wanted to learn.'

Proving he wasn't, he retorted, 'Well, now's your chance.'

While Rider lit a couple of oil lamps and adjusted the tall glass chimneys, she noticed the towel and soap he'd put on the sink and went over to wash her hands. Some energetic pumping produced only clanking and asthmatical wheezes.

'You'll need to prime it,' he said.

Dita was a city girl born and bred. Black brows drawn together in a frown, she echoed, 'Prime it? I've no idea how to do that.'

'Pour some water into it.'

She hugged herself before asking innocently, 'You have brought some water?'

'Of course.'

'Clever Dick,' she muttered beneath her breath, then started as he appeared at her side holding a plastic bottle.

After he'd primed it and worked the handle, the pump gave a triumphant gurgle and began to spew out clear, icy cold water. By the time Dita's hands were clean they were also numb.

As he fastened the internal shutters over the windows, closing out the snowy dusk and leaving the room bathed in yellow lamplight, she rooted in her case, which he'd hefted on to a wooden bunk built against the far wall.

Shivering, she hastily changed into trousers and a jumper, noting for the first time how small the bunk seemed. It was not only narrow, but short, totally inadequate for a man of Rider's height. 'Hoist with his own petard', she thought gleefully.

'What are you grinning about?' His sudden question made her jump.

She was debating the wisdom of telling him, when he said, 'I take it the deficiencies of the bed are amusing you?'

Her voice dripping with sympathy, she observed, 'I'm afraid you won't be getting much sleep.'

'I wasn't planning to.'

His soft rejoinder made every nerve in her body tingle into life and her heart begin to race. As he approached she stood rooted to the spot, at the mercy of all the sensations he always aroused in her. He tilted her face up to his, leaving her nowhere to hide from his hard, too perceptive gaze.

She looked at him, her heart thumping, her eyes wide, her beautiful lips parted slightly, waiting eagerly for his kiss.

Pulling a spotless hankie from his pocket, he held it to her mouth and instructed, 'Spit.'

When she just stared at him blankly, his smile mocking, he said, 'You've a streak of soot across your cheek, and this way has to be warmer than the pump.'

She spat, and he wiped her face before replacing the hankie and moving away. Heart still thudding uncomfortably, hands unsteady, she cursed her own vulnerability while she unpinned Rider's orchid and put her wedding outfit away in her case. There appeared to be no storage space for clothes, so the phrase 'living out of a suitcase' took on a whole new meaning.

Though the range was soon blazing merrily and throwing out a comforting heat, beyond the circle of warmth the air remained so chill that, despite feeling she'd been transported back to pioneering days, Dita was glad to be doing the cooking.

Having changed into casual trousers and a black crewnecked sweater, Rider busied himself removing the cork from a bottle of Californian Cabernet Sauvignon and setting it to warm. Then, his sleeves rolled up to expose muscular arms, he employed a bucket to fill the range's capacious boiler, remarking as he did so, 'We'll have a plentiful supply of hot water by bedtime.'

While mushrooms simmered in a cream sauce and a couple of steaks sizzled and spat over the bars of the grill, Dita found tin cutlery and thick plates and set the bare, scrubbed table. With a touch of grim humour she put the orchid in an empty margarine carton and lit a candle by way of decoration.

'Very tasteful,' he approved.

'I'm afraid the wine glasses lower the tone somewhat . . .'

Rider cocked an eyebrow at the brown pottery mugs.

'. . . but it was either those or plastic cups.'

'Oh, mugs every time,' he agreed.

Suddenly she began to laugh, laughter that was quite genuine but also, after such a fraught day, perilously close to tears. Realising the danger, she pulled herself up short and spluttered, 'Your friends... if they could see you now... jet-setter Rider Barron on honeymoon!'

His teeth flashed in a white grin. 'It may not be the Waldorf Astoria, but the men at least would envy me.'

Showing how starved she was for some sign that he still found her attractive, she was grateful for even that small crumb.

The meal turned out to be surprisingly good and, having eaten hardly anything at lunch, Dita tucked in with a will. She felt absurdly pleased and gratified when Rider smiled and lifted his mug to toast, 'Perdita, a born backwoods cook.'

By the time they were finished, the old black kettle, which she'd filled and placed on the hob, was singing merrily, steam rattling its lid.

When they'd drunk their coffee, Rider pulled a couple of shabby but comfortable armchairs up to the warmth and, firelight glowing on their faces, they sat sipping brandy. But though the cosy scene should have been relaxed and intimate Dita was aware of a growing tension.

Wanting to break the silence, which was becoming more strained by the minute, she asked, 'I take it we've got a bathroom?'

'Oh, yes, we've got a bathroom,' he answered, his determinedly light tone matching hers. 'It's through that door. Not many mod cons, but plenty of ventilation.'

Visualising the rickety lean-to she'd glimpsed earlier, Dita shuddered and said in a heartfelt tone, 'I bet.'

Rider gave a short sharp sigh and admitted, 'I'm being a swine to you, aren't I? But we needn't stay if you don't want to.'

She considered. 'I think I do want to.' Despite the spartan conditions, it was preferable to a hotel. In fact as far as she was concerned the only thing needed to make it perfect was for Rider to soften, to show some warmth and kindness, some desire for her.

To prevent the silence closing in again, she asked, 'Apart from wanting to pay me back for... shall we say... my aversion to honeymoons, what made you choose this cabin? How did a city man like you come to know about it?'

'Ah, but I'm not a city man. You see, my parents never wanted me, they had no time for a baby...' His voice was flat, dispassionate, but beneath that matter-of-fact statement she could sense that his parental rejection had caused a deep and lasting hurt.

'Even as a young man my father was too busy following the political trail, and my mother was too busy following him, so I lived with my grandparents at Rider's Keep until I went to university.

'My grandfather, another Rider, loved to be outdoors, and in summer we spent all our spare time climbing, trekking, swimming, or canoeing. In winter we chopped wood, skied cross-country and snow-mobiled. Often we stayed in this very cabin. Then it belonged to Walt Delaney, a friend of my grandfather's. Now it belongs to Walt's son.'

That brief account of his childhood explained a lot of things and added a whole new dimension to his character, Dita thought. But one thing didn't quite add up. 'I understood you'd only bought Rider's Keep fairly recently?'

'Yes, that's right. My grandmother died while I was still at Columbia, and my grandfather a year or so later. He'd always intended to leave the house to me, but he'd neglected to make a will to that effect, so it went to my father.

'While I was on an extended business trip to Europe and Asia he sold it, in spite of knowing I was in the process of releasing funds to buy it.' Now Rider made no attempt to hide the bitterness. 'I approached the new owner but, understandably, he refused to part with it. However, he promised me first refusal if it ever went on the market again. It was seven years before it did.'

'And though you've got the house back you still haven't forgiven your father,' she said slowly.

'Ah, now you've uncovered the blackest part of my character. I don't find it easy to forgive sheer bloody-mindedness...'

She shivered, as if someone had danced on her grave. If he couldn't bring himself to forgive his own father, how could she hope that he'd ever forgive *her*?

As if reading her mind, he added, 'Or lack of trust.' The last was spoken with a lethal softness that made her flinch as though he'd struck her.

Clearly it had been a bitter blow to him. He'd *expected* her to trust him.

But to expect to be trusted, surely a man had to know himself trustworthy, otherwise he would be the worst kind of hypocrite. And, whatever his faults, Rider was no hypocrite; that she was certain of.

Nor was he a man who lied, or lacked self-control.

So could she have made a terrible mistake? Had she been wrong to believe the worst?

To begin with she'd trusted him blindly, and would have gone on trusting him if he hadn't admitted everything. That was the stumbling-block. No matter how much she wanted to believe she'd made a mistake, he'd *admitted* to being Julie Dawn's lover. It always came back to that.

A barely audible sigh drifted from her lips, and she leaned her head against the back of the chair while she stared into the flames.

She felt an ache in her heart, a poignant regret for what might have been between them, if a lack of trust on her part, and a bitter resentment on his, hadn't set them on opposite sides of an abyss. An abyss which, despite his admitted obsession for her, and her feelings for him, it seemed impossible to bridge.

But there *had* to be a way. Physical closeness would hopefully provide a starting-point, a foundation they could build on. Surely when they were making love, lying in each other's arms, he couldn't remain mentally at a distance?

Or could he? Remembering with a dart of pain how he'd reacted last time, she wasn't so confident. Still, she must hold on to the hope.

After a while the combination of brandy and warmth made her drowsy, and, stifling a yawn, she asked, 'Isn't it about time for bed?'

Without moving, he said, 'Better watch it; you're giving the impression of an eager bride.'

Hating the sarcasm in his voice, she retorted, 'And you've giving the impression of a reluctant groom.'

'Perhaps that's what I am.'

A chill running through her, she thought of how remote he'd seemed during the preceding days, how he'd avoided contact with her and kept her at arm's length. Raggedly, she said, 'I can't understand why you went through with this wedding if you don't even want me any longer.'

'Let's say I want more than you can give.'

'I...I don't understand what you mean,' she whispered.

'You warned me it would be a forced marriage, but when we made our "bargain" I was too obsessed to care. Now I find that knowing my bride feels nothing but a reluctant determination to fulfil her part of the bargain isn't much of an aphrodisiac.'

'There's nothing reluctant about it.'

'Perhaps the trouble is I don't want determination either.'

'Then what do you want?'

He laughed with disgust and self-derision. 'The impossible. I want to wipe out the last few years as if they'd never been. I want to walk into Ryan's and find you sitting behind your office desk, as untouched by tragedy, as innocent as you were before you loved and married Stephen.'

Unbearably affected by his words, she said unsteadily, 'There can't be many people who at some time in their lives don't want to wipe out the past and start again. But, as you said yourself, it isn't possible.'

'No,' he admitted, 'the past always leaves an indelible mark. Past mistakes, past failures...' He sounded both bitter and frustrated.

'But we can make the best of the present.' She spoke with more confidence than she felt.

'I've told myself that repeatedly, but I can't stomach the thought of three in a bed.'

She stared at him blankly. 'What do you mean, three in a bed?'

'The third one being a ghost. I saw how much you loved your husband. You suffered for him, worked yourself to a shadow for him... I was a fool to think you might have got over it. Love like that doesn't fade or die...'

Dita made a movement of protest but, ignoring it, Rider went on, 'It took me a long time to realise why you were so set against having a honeymoon. Too long. Not until after the ceremony, and I saw the look on your face when Kate brought the subject up.

'"Honeymoons can be so public"... that's what you first told me. You didn't want to go to a hotel, to be among people, to have an audience. Stuck with a husband you *didn't* love, and memories of one you *did*, what could be worse than having to act the part of a happy bride?'

Vehemently, she said, 'You're completely wrong.'

Brushing her denial aside, he smiled crookedly. 'It serves me right. When I realised the kind of situation you were in after your husband died, I deliberately set out to trap you.'

'It might have been deliberate, but at least you were honest. I *wanted* to help Paul's family, and at the very least I owe you——'

Roughly, he broke in, 'If you'd said no deal and stuck to it, I would have helped the Wilsons regardless, out of sheer humanity, so forget it, you don't owe me a thing. I had no right to try and take your husband's place.'

Now knowing that she was fighting, aware that the whole of their future together might depend on her being able to make Rider believe her, Dita said urgently, 'What I do or don't owe you has absolutely nothing to do with it. Please listen... I want to tell you about Stephen and me. About our relationship...'

CHAPTER EIGHT

SEEING she had Rider's attention, Dita began to speak, choosing her words with care. 'After lunch today, while we were freshening up, Kate talked about feeling guilty. She said something about guilt keeping you awake at night and burning into your soul. Though on one hand I don't know what she meant, on the other I know *exactly*, and she's perfectly right.'

Lifting his head, he objected roughly, 'I'm sure you can't feel any guilt as far as your husband's concerned.'

'Wrong again.'

'What have you to feel guilty about?'

'I didn't love him, or at least not the way he wanted me to.'

As though she'd dropped a bombshell, Rider sat quite motionless staring at her.

Swallowing, she went on, 'I was fond of Stephen and I respected him, but I didn't love him in the way a wife should love her husband. He wanted me to, and lord knows, I tried. But no one can love to order...

'When he asked me to marry him, I told him the truth, but he said that he loved me and if I was fond of him that would be enough. But it wasn't.'

'There's something I don't understand...' Rider's face was taut, as though he was under a great emotional strain. 'If things were as you say, and you didn't love Stephen, why were you so reluctant to come away on honeymoon with me?'

'My first honeymoon was——'

121

'When I asked if you'd had a previous honeymoon, you said no,' Rider broke in, his voice cold and brittle as ice.

'That wasn't what you asked,' she objected quietly. 'You remarked—sardonically, I might add—that a honeymoon was a time for soft lights and sweet music, romance and love. Then you said, "Didn't you enjoy that euphoric start to marriage last time?" That was the question I answered no to.'

'Isn't that rather splitting hairs, Perdita?'

'I don't think so.'

'Very well, go on and tell me about it.'

She hesitated, reluctant to bring her guilt into the open. It was almost as though, if she didn't admit it, it wouldn't be true, wouldn't exist.

But perhaps she should tell him, tell him everything and get it over with?

No! a warning voice screamed through her brain. The moment wasn't right. She needed more time to try to establish a stable relationship before telling him the whole truth.

Taking a deep, steadying breath, she said, 'Although we couldn't really afford a honeymoon, Stephen wanted us to have one, so we did. But it...it didn't work out.'

Feeling ill and on edge, she'd found the week at Niagara Falls an absolute nightmare. Though she could hardly admit that to Rider, without revealing facts she preferred to keep hidden.

Gritting her teeth, she added, 'The thing is, it was all my fault, and just the mention of the word "honeymoon" brought back so many memories of guilt and failure.'

'Why in God's name did you marry him if you didn't love him?' Rider demanded.

But that was one thing she couldn't tell him.

As she hesitated, he said urgently, 'I *need* to understand. Need to know *why*, *how* it happened. Perhaps then I can come to terms with it, stop torturing myself.'

'I don't know where to start,' she said helplessly.

He was in no doubt. 'Start from when I left for San Francisco.'

The controlled line of her mouth testifying to the tight hold she was keeping on her emotions, Dita pretended to think about that day. In truth, she didn't need to; it was engraved on her heart.

Her voice quiet but clear, she began, 'You know Stephen lived in the apartment above mine? We'd spoken briefly to each other when we happened to meet, but the first time we really talked was that Friday night.

'I was just arriving home from work when he came by and enquired if I'd got a phone. When I told him I hadn't, he said he'd have a pizza at Joe's and phone from there. Then he asked me if I'd like to join him; he said he needed cheering up...'

'So that's why you weren't home Friday night,' Rider murmured, as though speaking to himself. Then more forcefully, 'Well, go on; why did he need cheering up?'

'He'd lost both his job and his girlfriend and, on top of that, his mother had had a stroke, so he'd decided to go home to Georgia for a while.

'I was genuinely sorry for him, but the only person I could think about was you. How soon you'd be home, when I'd see you again...

'Then the next morning I read in the paper that you'd admitted to being Julie Dawn's lover.' For the first time her voice faltered. 'It was like being hit by a hurricane. My whole life smashed into bits in a few seconds.'

She shuddered with the force of the emotions that ran through her. At one time she'd thought those emotions dead, battered to death. But they hadn't died.

After a second or two she forced herself to go on. 'I was still sitting there stunned when Stephen knocked at the door to say goodbye. When he realised how... upset I was, he refused to leave me.

'He wanted to know what I intended to do, but I had no idea. My only clear thought was that I couldn't bear to see you again. I had to get away from New York before you came back.'

His voice as bleak as the Arctic, Rider asked, 'You didn't even consider waiting to hear what I might have to say?'

Her instinct was to defend herself, but she ignored it, and tried instead to face the truth. 'Though I'd always believed I trusted you, subconsciously, I suppose, I'd been almost *waiting* for you to live up to your playboy image. I had so little confidence in my ability to hold you, so many doubts about fitting into your life in any permanent way, that I'd half expected to lose you.'

Rider's hands were clenched on the arms of his chair, his knuckles gleaming white. 'So I take it you went to Georgia?'

'Yes.' Her voice was scarcely above a whisper. 'When I said I wanted to leave New York, Stephen suggested I accompany him.'

'As what? His wife? His mistress?'

She shook her head. 'No, only a friend. Though I didn't tell him anything except I'd lost the man I... any details... he knew I'd had a bad shock and he was just being kind.' And was already half in love with her, prepared to wait...though he hadn't told her that until later.

'He was planning to stay with his mother, and he said it would be an ideal solution if I stayed there too. That way I'd have time to sort out my life, and she wouldn't be left alone while he was working.

'I didn't like leaving Tim Ryan in the lurch, but I wrote out my resignation and Stephen put it in the mail and phoned his mother while I packed. My rent was paid up until the end of the month, so all I needed to do was hand in my keys. Before eleven o'clock we were on a bus bound for Atlanta.'

'So Kate must have just missed you.'

'Kate?' Dita was perplexed. 'Why was Kate calling on me?'

Ignoring her question, Rider said tersely, 'Tell me what happened when you got to Atlanta.'

'The house Mrs West rented was white clapboard, charmingly "southern", with a veranda and a magnolia tree in the garden. It wasn't very big but it did have three bedrooms, and she was kindness itself to me. She was very like her son, both in looks and character.

'Stephen, who was a trained chef, was lucky enough to get a job in one of the Degg Baker hotels, and I did the housework and kept his mother company.'

Dita bit her lip, then went on, 'We'd only been there for a couple of months when Mrs West had another stroke. She was dead before we reached hospital.

'The landlord wanted us out of the house, and we were looking for somewhere else to live when the chain Stephen worked for offered him a job in one of their New York hotels...'

Rider was listening with strained attention, his face set, his gaze direct and dissecting.

'He wanted to take it, he loved what he called the real bright lights, so we went back. We had no money and no place to live, but the hotel provided accommodation for married staff...' Her voice tailed off at the sudden blaze in Rider's grey eyes.

'Don't tell me that was the only reason you got married!' he burst out.

Somehow she answered, 'No, it wasn't the only reason. He...he loved me and I liked him very much.' Flatly, she added, 'It seemed the best thing to do.'

Rider's expression unnerved her; it was full of impotent rage. 'I could have understood it if you'd been passionately in love, but to marry him in those circumstances...'

Knowing she mustn't let him suspect the truth, and afraid of his quick, analytical mind, she said quickly, 'I'd had enough of being passionately in love. I'd been passionately in love with you, and where had that got me...? All I wanted was kindness and security, and Stephen offered me both.'

Like a shutter coming down, hiding what he was thinking, feeling, Rider's face went as blank as any robot's. After a moment he remarked coldly, 'I'm not sure I like this scenario any better than the other.'

Realising that her chance of making things come right between them was slipping away, Dita decided on shock tactics and, jumping to her feet, let fly. 'You really are the giddy limit,' she raged at him. 'When you thought I loved Stephen it didn't suit you, and now you know the truth you're still not satisfied!'

He looked at her, startled into becoming human once more. Her heart lifting, she continued her tirade. 'I'm beginning to think the whole thing's nothing but an excuse to save you having to make love to me... Don't you want me any more? Am I *so* unattractive?'

'You were always hauntingly beautiful, Perdita.' His usually clear, crisp voice was husky. 'But now you've an added poignancy that makes you exquisite.'

'Then what's the matter?' she taunted. 'Have you suddenly become impotent?'

His eyes glinted dangerously. 'Do you want me to prove I haven't?'

Boldly she went and sat on his knee. Putting her arms around his neck, she pressed her lips against his throat, and urged, 'Yes, please.' She felt him swallow convulsively before his arms closed around her.

For a few seconds he just held her, then he began to kiss her as if he'd waited all his life for this moment. He kissed her temples, her closed eyelids, her cheeks and chin, and finally, with a rare sweetness, a promise of delight, an eroticism that set her aflame, her mouth.

Indicating her trousers and jumper, he said thickly, 'Take them off.'

Gladly, she obeyed, and he settled her back on his knee. As she nestled against him, feeling the heat of the fire on her bare skin, he began to take the pins from her hair. When it fell in a long, fragrant swath he buried his face in the silken mass before starting to kiss her again, deep, seductive kisses that were as welcome as sweet water to someone who had just crossed a desert.

While, with masterful tenderness, he used his hands and lips to stimulate and excite her, she let her own hands travel beneath his sweater to trace bone and muscle and sinew. Revelling in the warmth of his smooth skin beneath her palms, delighting in their closeness after the previous desolation, she knew she'd never felt so satisfied and happy.

She must have spoken the thought aloud, because Rider said, 'In just a little while I intend to make you even happier and a great deal more satisfied.'

Elation bubbling inside her like a joyful fountain, she grinned and, deliberately sceptical, murmured, 'Do you think you can?'

'Woman,' Rider drawled threateningly, 'how dare you cast aspersions on my prowess as a lover?' He nuzzled her flimsy bra aside and gave her a love-bite, while his fingers smoothed over her ribcage. 'I'll have you know that, with the maximum temptation and the right to gratify it, before the honeymoon's over I may well become a sexual athlete.'

She grinned again, enchantingly. 'Thinking of that bunk, rather than a sexual athlete you'll need to become a contortionist.'

'Ah, but I *wasn't* thinking of the bunk. I have other and, I hope, better plans.'

'Not a snowdrift!' she exclaimed. 'But then I really don't think...' Her words ended in a gasping giggle as he found a ticklish spot.

Hand poised menacingly, he asked softly, 'What don't you think, Perdita?'

She caught hold of his wrist. 'If you stop it, I might tell you.'

'Only might?'

His fingers resumed their tormenting, evoking a squeak and a breathless surrender. 'All right, I *will*...' Her voice low and not quite steady, she said, 'I don't think I mind where you make love to me, whether it's in a snowdrift or that ridiculous bunk, so long as you do.'

She heard the hiss of his breath and passion darkened his eyes to charcoal. In contrast his words were deliberately mundane. 'Well, first I'll get you something warm to put on while I make a few preparations.'

Comfortably clad in her cuddly, teddy-bear-coloured dressing-gown, and furry slippers, Dita opened the far door and peered cautiously into the cold lean-to. In the gloom she saw that besides a chemical-flush toilet it boasted a wash-basin with a plug dangling from a length of rusty chain, and what appeared to be a shower, though there was no sign of any running water.

Having cleaned her teeth in the main sink, she used a metal dipper like a huge soup ladle to fill a plastic bucket with hot water from the range's boiler. Then, disregarding her flimsy honeymoon nightdress as hardly suitable and choosing instead an apricot-coloured brushed nylon, she collected her toilet-bag and towel, picked up one of the oil lamps and, feeling like Florence Nightingale, ventured into the 'bathroom'.

Several pairs of skis, a sledge, and some snow-shoes were propped against one of the walls, along with a fascinating selection of boots, jackets, hats, helmets, scarves, mittens and goggles.

On the opposite wall hung two zinc-coated bath-tubs, one large, the other quite small. If there had been one in between they could have belonged to the three bears, she thought with a smile.

Icy cold blasts blowing through gaps in the boarding made her ablutions skimpy, and, teeth chattering, she was glad to hurry back to the fire.

In the relatively short space of time she'd been gone, a bed had appeared in front of the glowing hearth. A luxurious double bed, with an inflated box-mattress, two plump pillows, a down sleeping-bag, and several soft blankets.

Two steaming mugs of cocoa were keeping warm on the range while, stripped to the waist, Rider was washing under the pump.

His waist narrow, his hips lean, he looked superbly fit and healthy, without an ounce of spare flesh. Watching the muscles rippling beneath the smooth olive skin of his broad back and shoulders, Dita felt her pulses quicken and her breath catch in her throat.

She was aware that he worked out in the hotel gym and used the pool regularly, but she'd often wondered how a townee came to have such a magnificent physique in the first place. Now, knowing the way he'd spent his boyhood, she no longer had to wonder.

Suddenly recalling what she had in her case for him, she retrieved it from the lid pocket and slid it under the nearest pillow just as, towelling himself, he returned to the fire, drops of water still trickling down his face and darkening the front of his thick blond hair.

They drank their cocoa sitting opposite each other, like Jack and Jill practising to be Darby and Joan. But beneath the surface calm a heated excitement simmered.

Determined, however, that this time *he* should make the first move, Dita sat quietly until he looked up, firelight dancing in his grey eyes, and said, 'Come here, Perdita.'

Reaching beneath the pillow for the flat packet she'd secreted there, she went and sat on his knee. 'This is for you. A wedding present.'

Though she hadn't intended it to, it was obvious that her unexpected gift had momentarily thrown him. Then, his surprise swiftly masked, he said levelly, 'I have something for you, but I haven't brought it with me.' After a moment he sighed. 'Perhaps I should tell you why——'

'You don't need to tell me why,' she interrupted tartly. 'I already know. You're practically paranoid when it comes to being thanked for anything.'

He seemed dumbstruck and, emboldened by his silence, she went on, 'Because of past mistakes we're in an intolerable position. You don't feel comfortable giving me anything, and I can't say a simple thank you without you suspecting me of sarcasm, or worse.'

There was a pregnant pause. Then, 'You're quite right,' Rider admitted, 'and it's my fault we're in that position. The way you thanked me that day after reading Mrs Wilson's letter...I felt so bloody guilty that it made the question of gratitude a rather sensitive issue...'

'Sensitive?' she mocked. 'Are you sure you don't mean explosive?'

He put his hand against her cheek and turned her face fully to his. His touch was light, in complete contrast to his intense expression. 'In future I'll try to behave more rationally.'

Moving her head a little, she kissed his palm, and saw his throat move as he swallowed hard. Keeping in check the feelings that threatened to swamp her, she indicated the package he was still holding and asked a shade unsteadily, 'Aren't you going to open it?'

Without further ado he tore off the plain dark blue paper and turned the slim book over in his hands. Entitled simply *Learning How To Fly*, it was a small masterpiece done in exquisite detail.

Its cover was a jewel-bright riot of colour as, from a green and gold rowan hung with scarlet berries, a nursery class of bare, roly-poly, mischievous baby fairies with gauzy-rainbow wings tumbled and flew, playing and laughing, while a flustered teacher tried vainly to keep them in order.

In the centre, a podgy little girl fairy trying to launch herself into space was being held back by a naughty little boy fairy grasping her wispy pigtail.

At the bottom of the tree one tiny, dimpled babe had curled up and gone to sleep, head pillowed on a tuft of grass, while close by a more adventurous tot with a snub nose and a crew-cut was attempting to ride an indignant-looking caterpillar.

Chuckling, Rider opened the book. His smile faded as he read the dedication—'For Rider'.

It was clear that he was moved, in the grip of some powerful emotion, but exactly *what* emotion she was unable to tell.

The long, painful pause convincing her that she'd made a bad mistake, Dita sighed inwardly, regretting, on more than one count, that she'd given it to him.

Without saying a syllable he slowly began to turn the pages, reading the short, simple stories, and looking at the delightfully humorous illustrations. At the very end was a picture of the fairy king sitting on a smooth grey rock, knees drawn up, magnificent wings folded.

Dita felt Rider freeze and held her breath, waiting for the explosion. Though the king's thick fair hair was adorned with a crown of trailing ivy and his ears had a tinge of green and were slightly pointed, there was no doubt whose face it was.

Suddenly Rider began to laugh helplessly, deep, *amused* laughter that rumbled and resounded in his chest, and made Dita know he wasn't angry with her.

Though he tried to pretend he was. 'Why, you little...!' he spluttered. 'I should take you over my knee for that.'

'I hadn't intended it to happen,' she explained, half apologetically. 'But on some level I must have been thinking about you and that's how it came out, so I decided to leave it.'

He gave another choke of laughter, before adding severely, 'And stark naked too.'

'But very proper,' she hastened to point out, adding after a moment, 'I'm glad you don't mind overmuch... When it was too late I couldn't help but wonder what you'd think.'

'I think you're marvellously talented,' he told her. 'And though I won't dare show my face in Manhattan for the next decade or so I'm enormously proud of you.'

'Then you won't mind if I go on writing?'

'Of course I won't mind. But if you're intending to stay on at Cromford's, when will you find time? I plan to be a very demanding husband.'

'I'm not going to stay on at Cromford's. You said you would prefer it if your wife didn't go out to work, so I handed in my notice. I'll have plenty to keep me occupied.'

'Mmm...' He kissed the warm hollow behind her ear. 'Certainly as far as the nights go. And speaking of nights... aren't we rather wasting this one?'

'I was wondering when we were going to get round to something more exciting than talking,' she informed him saucily.

Laughing, he stood up with her in his arms, and said, 'Well, if it's excitement you're looking for...'

She lay in bed and waited while he doused the oil lamps, then, her heart racing with suffocating speed, she watched him remove the rest of his clothes before joining her. In the fire-glow, with his hawk-like features, his clean, powerful body-lines and golden-bronze skin, he looked like some Aztec god.

Masterful, yet at the same time heartbreakingly tender, he made a wonderful lover. Together, as one, they shared the joyful contact of hands and lips and bodies, the escalating pleasure, then the sudden and blinding explosion of delight and ecstasy.

As their breathing slowed and returned to normal, he lifted himself away and lay by her side, still and quiet. When he made no move to hold her close, she snuggled against him as though for warmth. He gave a kind of sigh and sat up to pull the blankets over them, remarking, 'When the stove dies down it will get even colder.'

'I'm not cold,' she said. 'But as it's my wedding night...'

In a goaded voice he said, 'Not your *first* wedding night...'

Her heart like lead, she asked, 'Do you mind so much?'

'Of course I mind. Fool that I am, I wanted to be your first lover and your last. The only man in your life. Can't you understand that?'

Drawing away from him, she said resentfully, 'Oh, yes, I understand very well. I wanted to be the only woman in your life. Even if I was just an ordinary working girl, I didn't want to play second fiddle to Julie Dawn.'

Despite the exchange of passion, all that had gone before, they were as far apart as ever, making her previous hope seen as fantastic, as insubstantial, as an ignis fatuus.

Next morning, surfacing slowly, she stirred and stretched, feeling drowsily warm and contented until she recalled the unhappy sequel to their lovemaking. Somehow, she resolved, they must get back on a friendlier footing.

Eyes still closed, she reached out her hand to touch Rider. But, as though history was repeating itself, he was gone, the bed beside her cool and empty.

Her lids flew open.

This time, however, he was quite close. Standing by the glowing range, fully dressed, he was turning sizzling bacon in a big black frying-pan, while a bubbling percolator filled the cabin with the delicious aroma of fresh coffee.

Aware of the movement, he turned his head and said lightly, casually, 'There's been a heavy fall of snow during the night, but it's a beautiful morning, blue skies and sunshine.'

Following his lead, she suggested equally lightly, 'Perhaps we can go out after breakfast? Skiing maybe?'

He raised an eyebrow. 'Do you ski?'

'Oh, yes,' she assured him airily.

'Well?'

Deliberately provocative, she said, 'I expect when I get into practice I'll be able to leave you standing.'

His grey eyes gleamed. 'Oh? Just how good are you?'

Black hair tousled, green eyes still sleepy, she grinned and admitted, 'I haven't learnt yet.'

'In that case it's high time you did.' Cheerfully callous, he added, 'You shouldn't fall down more than a couple of dozen times before you get the hang of it.'

In mock-alarm, she protested, 'Perhaps I should reconsider. Suppose I end up covered with bruises?'

'I'll kiss every one individually,' he promised.

She grinned. 'That's a bold statement, considering where the majority are likely to be.'

The day was as lovely as Rider had said, and the mountain scenery quite spectacular. The nearest dwelling turned out to be in the village, two or three kilometres away, and the only people they saw were distant skiers.

Once she got the feel of the skis strapped to her feet, and Rider had demonstrated the correct stance and the basics, being blessed with a good sense of balance she soon proved herself a natural.

Wary of her overdoing it, however, Rider refused to let her attempt anything too strenuous, and when they returned to the cabin after a couple of hours she had nothing to complain of except a slight stiffness.

Even that had its compensations, as Rider produced some oil from the medicine chest and proceeded to massage her with a dedication and an expertise that soon made her forget the original purpose of the exercise.

Later, when Dita remarked a shade wistfully that it would be lovely to have a hot bath, Rider carried in the largest of the galvanised tubs, and began to fill it from the boiler.

While he topped it up from time to time with a steaming kettle, she enjoyed the sybaritic luxury of a leisurely bath in front of a blazing fire, and then the pleasurable excitement of being masterfully, and erotically, dried from head to toe.

On a purely physical level they were totally in tune. By tacit consent they avoided talking of anything controversial and isolated themselves in a kind of halcyon bubble, cut off from both past and future, refusing to think beyond the present.

On Christmas Eve they collected holly and ivy and pine cones to decorate the cabin, and Rider cut a spruce branch in place of a tree. Trimmed with cotton-wool snow and bunches of scarlet berries, a silver star fashioned from kitchen foil fastened to the top, it served the purpose very well.

On Christmas morning they drank Bucks Fizz in bed and, as their present to each other, made love until lunchtime.

The weather staying good, with cloudless skies and only a couple of light sprinkles of overnight snow, they spent most of their days outdoors. In the evenings they sat round the range, sometimes reading, other times playing checkers, and toasted chestnuts or pink and white marshmallows.

A couple of times, while Dita prepared lunch, Rider donned a rucksack and skied to the nearby village for bread and fresh milk.

They saw the New Year in with champagne and, the crisp winter air having given them both an excellent appetite, treated themselves to a midnight feast of crackers and caviare and smoked salmon sandwiches.

Then suddenly the honeymoon was over.

While Dita swept and tidied, Rider cleared the snow from the car, packed the trunk, and fitted snow-chains.

All too soon it was time to lock up the cabin and head for home, time to acknowledge the past and face the future, to test their magic bubble in the everyday world.

They negotiated the track without difficulty and joined the serpentine road which wound down the hill, but even with the chains the big car slipped and slithered on the first steep bend, causing an involuntary gasp to leave Dita's lips.

Since the accident—though she usually managed to hide it—she'd tended to be nervous, and now the circumstances made her even more so.

Rider shot her a quick glance, and remarked reassuringly, 'We'll be fine as soon as we hit the valley highway. Chains feel awkward when you're not used to them, but I'm familiar with these sort of conditions and I know how to cope, so don't be afraid.'

'I'm not afraid,' she denied quickly. 'I trust you implicitly.' The second they were spoken she regretted her unthinking choice of words, but it was too late.

He stiffened abruptly and his grey eyes emptied of all warmth. Bleakly, he said, 'If only that were true.'

The bubble had burst.

CHAPTER NINE

IT WAS fair when they started off, but as they headed out of the Catskills the day became greyer, with puffs of dark cloud drifting across the sky like smoke signals. Soon it began to spit with a mixture of snow and rain. By the time they stopped for a late lunch at a wayside inn, heavy sleet was falling.

Manhattan proved to be cold, wet, and dreary, with muddy slush underfoot and an unmistakable post-Christmas-New Year depression; window displays that were no longer relevant, and bedraggled decorations hanging around like weary ghosts left too long at a party.

In contrast, Markman's, with its calm bustle of activity, its blazing fires and bowls of spring flowers, looked a great deal more cheerful and inviting.

The news of their marriage having spread like wildfire, they were greeted by the staff with smiling good wishes and given, along with their mail, several small gifts. In addition, a beautiful basket of hothouse blooms, accompanied by a huge congratulations card signed by the entire workforce, was waiting for them.

Standing in Rider's attractive lounge, Dita felt suddenly lost, out of place, as discomfited as a visitor unsure of her welcome and uncertain what to do next.

'Not quite home yet?' Rider queried perceptively.

'I'm sure it soon will be,' she said firmly. 'It just seems strange not to be going into my own place.'

Making a positive effort to throw off the malaise, she went through to the master bedroom to find that, presumably on his instructions, all her clothes and personal belongings had been moved in and neatly put away.

Not one to leave tasks, she had almost finished her unpacking when Rider strolled through, and remarked, 'You look a little tired.'

'I am,' she admitted.

He studied her thoughtfully. 'And depressed?'

She nodded, and said with forced cheerfulness, 'Post-honeymoon blues. I expect things will look brighter in the morning.' But his earlier remark about trust was still weighing heavily on her spirits.

He came up from behind and, crossing his arms in front of her, drew her back against him and nuzzled her hair aside to kiss the warmth of her nape. 'Rather than going out, shall we have dinner sent up?'

His touch, his nearness, made her melt as always, while his caress sent little shivers of pleasure running through her. A shade unsteadily she said, 'That sounds like a good idea.'

'But first...' Releasing her, he went over to a small combination wall safe, hidden behind a pink and gold Matisse, and, having opened it, took out a ring which he slipped on to her wedding-finger.

It was a large, square-cut emerald in a plain gold setting which only served to enhance the wonderful clarity of the stone. So pure it was, so perfect, that she gazed at its glittering beauty as though hypnotised.

'You can thank me if you want to,' Rider said drily.

The ring must have cost a king's ransom, and was the loveliest thing she was ever likely to own, but she would have willingly exchanged it for the knowledge that he cared for her.

She lifted eyes the same exquisite colour as the jewel and, feeling the prick of tears, wordlessly wound her arms around his neck and stood on tiptoe to kiss him.

For a second or two his lips were firm and cool beneath hers, then as her own lips parted invitingly he deepened the kiss, sending her pulses racing, and making quivers of desire start in the pit of her stomach.

His lips moved over the clean line of her jaw and beneath her chin, tongue-tip lightly touching and tracing, then lingered to explore the warm hollow at the base of her throat while he dealt with blouse buttons and bra fastening.

Having bared her small but firm and beautifully shaped breasts, he paused to feast his eyes on them, before removing her green cords and briefs. Then, holding her in front of him, he turned her to face the tall cheval-glass.

Reflected in the mirror she saw her own slender body with its smooth, creamy skin, and over her shoulder Rider's hawk-like face. She watched his dark, powerful hands cupping and weighing her breasts, his thumbs delicately stimulating the pink nipples. Then while one hand continued its delightful torment the other travelled over the flat plane of her abdomen, to stroke and tug lightly at the dark silky curls.

Somehow, *seeing* what he was doing to her, as well as feeling, made it twice as erotic, and she dragged in her breath as though she'd been running.

Before she realised how far he was going to take it, she was caught up in mounting waves of pure pleasure. She tried to stop him then, but he was too strong for her and held her easily until he'd accomplished his purpose and she was taut and shuddering, consumed by sensation.

Her head fell back on his shoulder and he held her against him until beneath his left hand her heartbeat steadied and slowed a little.

Aware of his arousal, she expected him to lead her to the bed, but instead he let her go and moved away, saying coolly, 'I'll ask for our meal to be brought up in about fifteen minutes.'

A dawning realisation of *why* he'd done what he had, exactly what had prompted his actions, made rage tighten around her throat like a hempen noose. 'You devil!' she choked out, as he reached the door. 'You did that on purpose.'

Turning, he lifted one fair, well-marked brow in mock-surprise. 'Don't tell me you didn't enjoy it?'

'You intended to shame and humiliate me.'

His grey eyes glittered. 'Don't be a fool. You're my wife.'

'That doesn't mean I can't be sexually humiliated.'

'I didn't intend to humiliate you, Perdita,' he said curtly. 'But neither did I intend to accept payment for the ring. A simple "thank you" would have sufficed.'

'*Payment*!' she cried furiously, and, dragging the ring from her finger, threw it in his face. 'I don't hold myself that cheap.'

He laughed harshly. 'You'll be telling me next you can't be bought... And we both know that's not true,' he ended cruelly.

When the door closed behind him she sank on to the edge of the bed and burst into tears of futile anger and regret. What he'd apparently taken as a duty kiss had been a quite spontaneous urge to touch her mouth to his, to be close to him and thank him in the nicest way possible.

Now, all the stresses and strains, the pent-up worries and uncertainties of the past weeks, found their release, and when Rider came in some ten minutes later it was to discover her huddled in a woebegone heap, tears still flooding from her swollen eyes.

With an incoherent murmur, he sat down beside her and drew her into his arms. Weakly, she fought him. 'Leave me alone; I *hate* you.'

'Do you?' He cradled her head against his chest and, his lips brushing her sweet-smelling hair, admitted, 'Well, I dare say I deserve it.'

There was a world of bitterness, of defeat, in his voice that instantly dissolved her remaining anger.

'No, I don't hate you,' she retracted in a muffled voice. 'Though there are times I *want* to.'

'Then I must make sure those times are a thing of the past.' Holding her a little away, he produced a handkerchief and wiped her blotched cheeks with a tenderness that almost brought on fresh tears. 'Come along, you feel chilled; wash your face and put on something warm; our meal's waiting.'

When she'd bathed her eyes in cold water and combed her hair, instead of getting dressed again she pulled on a nightdress and the fluffy robe that was both comfortable and comforting.

On her way to the living-room, her slippered foot touched the ring still lying there. Picking it up, she returned it to her finger.

He noticed immediately. Raising her hand to his lips, he kissed it. 'No more misunderstandings?'

'That depends entirely on you.'

'Lay it on the line, Perdita.'

She did. 'You could try making a totem-pole from that chip on your shoulder.'

All at once he laughed with genuine amusement. 'What made you specify a totem-pole? Is it because you regard me as a savage?'

'No. Despite your fair hair I've always thought you had an Indian-type bone-structure.'

'How very perceptive of you. My grandmother had some Navajo blood.'

Interested, Dita begged, 'Tell me about it.'

'The Navajo were a tribe of Native Americans who lived and traded down in New Mexico. My grandmother's grandmother, whose name was Suni, was the only daughter of Chief Ramah. She was a girl respected and revered for her beauty and intelligence, and the pride of her father's heart, despite the fact that she defied him and married a white man.'

Grey eyes glinting wickedly, he added, 'So your suggestion was quite appropriate. But what if, instead of making a totem-pole, I use this—er—chip to fuel our mutual passion?'

Thinking of past conflagrations, she said in a heartfelt tone, 'Well, all I can say is, you'd better keep a fire-extinguisher handy.'

And during the following weeks she knew her comment had been a judicious one. He only had to touch her to send her up in flames, flames which engulfed and consumed them both.

But though he made love to her with an overwhelming passion, a masterful tenderness that left her senses reeling and her body singing with joyful satisfaction, mentally there was still a yawning chasm between them.

Once or twice a week she joined Rider for lunch, and most evenings they went out. They dined in fashionable restaurants, enjoyed films and concerts, plays and Broadway shows, went to ball-games and galleries, nightclubs and parties.

Rather than the settled contentment of marriage, it had the slightly frenzied feel of a high-powered love-affair. Yet no word of love was ever spoken, and beneath the whirl of activity lay a curious emptiness. A waiting.

It was one Friday afternoon towards the end of February before Dita, having had no contact with Kate, decided on the spur of the moment to ring Washington.

She felt restless and on edge, with time still to kill before she could make the phone call that dominated her thoughts. The call that would give her the results of the tests she'd undergone at Dr Wiseman's Clinic the previous day. Tests that, fearing her optimism might be misplaced, she had told Rider nothing about.

Having made herself a cup of tea, she drank it while she looked for the Barrons' number, flicking one-handed through the pad that lay by the phone.

The pages opened at D, and she was turning back to B when she caught sight of an entry that stopped her dead. Scrawled in Rider's strong black hand was the name Julie Dawn, followed by an address on West 34th, and a phone number.

Dita put her cup down with a little crash, and, her heart beating in slow, heavy thuds, stared at the damning evidence as though will-power alone could erase it, blot it out of the book and out of her memory.

Damning evidence, had been her first thought. But evidence of *what* exactly?

Taking a deep breath, she made a determined effort to calm herself. Finding the entry proved just one thing: that Rider had noted Julie Dawn's address and telephone number. It didn't prove their affair was still going on.

After a moment or two, hands steady now, she began to turn the pages once more and soon found the number she was seeking. In a few seconds, the connection made, she heard a clear, melodic voice answer, 'Kate Barron speaking.'

'Hi! This is Dita. If the mountain won't come to Muhammad... Or is it the other way around?'

Sounding flustered rather than pleased, Kate said, 'Oh, hi! How are you?'

'Fine, thanks. Did you have a good holiday?'

'Yes, Hawaii was very nice. Plenty of sunshine...'

They talked for a moment or two, Kate seeming so *distrait* that Dita asked, 'Have I rung at a bad time? Would it be better if I called back?'

'No...no, there's no need, really.'

'Only after the wedding, you mentioned a heart-to-heart...'

'Oh... Well, I...I really can't think at the moment what it was supposed to be about...' There was a pause, then she asked hesitantly, 'Is everything all right?'

Frowning, Dita asked, 'In what way?'

'I mean between you and Rider.'

Intending to assure her that everything was fine, Dita found herself blurting out, 'When I was looking for your number I found Julie Dawn's number and address.' Hastily, she added, 'I know it doesn't *mean* anything but...'

'Of course it doesn't,' Kate said, much too heartily, 'not a thing... Oh, by the way, Rider told me you've had a book published...'

Just the previous day, Dita had remarked on the fact that they hadn't heard from Washington, but Rider had said nothing about having been in touch.

Totally flummoxed, both by Kate's manner and the fact that Rider had apparently talked secretly to his step-mother, Dita let the other woman say goodbye and ring off without attempting to detain her.

There was no doubt in Dita's mind that Kate was pre-varicating because she no longer wanted to open her heart. Or had she been warned against it?

Remembering Rider's sharp glance when, as the older pair were leaving the Owl Inn, she'd mentioned a heart-

to-heart, Dita felt sure that *he* was the one who had
vetoed it. He'd known his stepmother could tell her
something he didn't want her to know. Something to do
with Julie Dawn, perhaps? Something that helped to
prove his guilt?

Making a great effort, Dita pushed the whole thing to
the back of her mind, and, dialling the number of the
gynaecological clinic, gave her name.

Hardly daring to believe it was true, she listened to
the nurse's cheerful voice saying, 'All the tests proved
positive, Mrs Barron.'

'You're sure?' It was little more than a croak.

'Quite sure. You seem to be as fit as a fiddle, and
everything looks fine, no problems. I've pencilled in an
appointment for next month's normal antenatal clinic...'

Like someone in a dream, Dita replaced the receiver,
and whispered, 'Thank you, God, oh, thank you.'

Yesterday she'd hardly dared hope; today, enveloped
in a rainbow cloud, her heart beating fast, she felt she
might burst with happiness and excitement.

Now that she had this wonderful news to redress the
sadness, it was time to tell Rider the truth. Tonight they
were going out, but later, when they went to bed and he
took her in his arms, she would tell him everything. That
done, they could make a new start with nothing to keep
them apart.

Except Julie Dawn.

But she wouldn't think about the address and phone
number she'd found on the pad, or Kate's strangeness.
She would clear her mind of all worries and let her new-
found happiness sink into her soul.

She was about to take a leisurely bath before getting
ready for the evening, when the phone rang.

Rider's low-pitched, decisive voice, said, 'Perdita, something important's cropped up, and I won't have time to get home. Can you take a cab to Pascal's?'

'Yes, of course.'

'I've booked a table for seven o'clock.'

'I'll be there.'

Yesterday at Pascal's was a comparatively new venture, but it was already well-known in the best circles for its superb cuisine and ambience. Characterised by a twenties décor, a postage-stamp-size dance-floor, and an orchestra that played the romantic melodies of Kern and Gershwin interspersed with the lively Charleston, it was *the* place to go.

Dita had one twenties-style dress in her wardrobe, a drop-waisted lilac georgette that contrived to be both loose and clinging at the same time. Matching satin pumps, and a long necklace of paler beads, completed the ensemble.

She swung her beads and did a short 'Thoroughly Modern Millie' routine, then, grinning at her reflection, decided that in order to really look the part she would need to be shingled. But Rider, who liked her black silky hair tumbling round her shoulders, would no doubt have something to say about that.

A glance at her watch making her realise she hadn't a lot of time, Dita hastily found a glittering evening bag with a silver chain, and donned a grey fur three-quarter-length coat.

On their return from honeymoon, Rider had wanted to buy her a mink, but she'd refused decidedly. When, a little nettled, he'd asked her why, she'd said calmly, 'Because I like animals,' and settled for a fun fur.

Though the night was cold it was fine and dry underfoot, and, her yellow cab having been caught in a solid-looking traffic jam at Fifth Avenue and 42nd Street,

Dita tapped on the plastic partition that separated the driver from his sometimes dangerous passengers, and got out.

Having peeled off some dollar bills to pay him, she returned the roll to her bag, pulled her coat around her and, knowing it would be considerably quicker, set off to walk the last block.

She'd almost reached the restaurant when a blow between her shoulder-blades sent her stumbling to her knees. As she threw out her hands to save herself, a darting figure made a clumsy attempt to snatch her bag.

Instinctively she clung to the chain, and as her assailant tried to wrench it free the bag came open, spilling its contents all over the pavement.

A car screeched to a halt by the kerb, and a man leapt out, making the would-be mugger abandon his attempt and turn to run. He'd only covered a short distance, however, when he was overtaken and ruthlessly floored.

Dita had struggled to her feet before she realised that her rescuer, who was returning dragging a tall, thin youth wearing trainers and a shabby anorak, was Rider.

'Are you all right?' he demanded urgently, holding his charge by the scruff of the neck.

Not altogether sure how she was, but wanting to reassure him, she answered breathlessly, 'Yes, I'm fine.'

Rider muttered something that could have been, 'Thank God.' Then he shook his captive the way a terrier shook a rat. 'If he'd hurt you...' Though the threat was left unfinished, apparently in fear for his life the youth began to whimper.

'No, no, he didn't hurt me,' she said quickly. 'I'm just a bit shaken. It was the suddenness of it.'

It had all happened in the twinkling of an eye. An isolated little incident that, despite heavy traffic and passing pedestrians, had attracted scarcely any atten-

tion. In a city where street scenes were commonplace
and violence was the norm, everyone looked the other
way, no one wanted to get involved.

'Don't call the cops,' the youth begged, wiping a trickle
of blood from the corner of his mouth with a torn sleeve.
'I've never been in trouble before.'

'Well, you are now.' Rider's face was steely. 'Deep
trouble.' Releasing his hold, he ordered curtly, 'Suppose
you pick up the lady's belongings?'

While Rider stood over him, the youth obeyed, shov-
elling everything back into Dita's bag and handing it to
her.

'I'm sorry, ma'am, I didn't mean to hurt you. I've
never hurt anyone in my life, at least not on purpose.
But I saw you pay the cabby... and I was desperate for
money.'

Dita, who knew what it was like to be desperate, felt
a quick sympathy for him.

'Which is it,' Rider queried bleakly, 'drink or drugs?'

'Neither, honest to God. It was food I wanted money
for. It's weeks since I had a proper meal. I've been living
out of trash cans.'

He was so hollow-eyed and gaunt it could well be the
truth, Dita thought. And he was pitifully young, no more
than sixteen or seventeen.

Rider studied him. 'What's your name?'

'Elmer Winkler.'

'That's not a New York accent.'

'I hitched from Virginia.'

'How long have you been here?'

'Mom died last month. I was on my own. I thought
New York would be easier. I thought I'd get a job...'

'A lot of people have made that mistake.' Rider
sounded far from charitable, but Dita, nothing if not
compassionate, was touched.

'Please, Rider...' She plucked at his sleeve.

Answering her unspoken appeal, he said curtly, 'You can thank your lucky stars firstly that my wife wasn't hurt, and secondly that she had a kind heart.' Reaching for his wallet, he produced a couple of ten-dollar bills and a slip of white pasteboard. 'Buy yourself a decent meal...' Cutting through the stammered thanks, he went on, 'And if you really want a job, bring that card to Markman's Hotel tomorrow morning and we'll have a talk.'

Apparently hardly able to believe his good fortune, the youth hurried away.

Rider put his arms around Dita and held her close, his cheek pressed against her hair. To her amazement she felt him shaking. His voice hoarse, almost incoherent, he muttered, 'I saw him hit you, and when you went down on your knees... For a minute I thought...' His arms tightened convulsively. 'Oh, dear God, he could have been holding a knife...'

'But he wasn't,' she said, determinedly cheerfully. 'It was just his fist. The only damage as far as I can tell is to my stockings.'

Feeling the shudders still running through Rider's big frame, she took the initiative. Lifting her head, she said, 'Come on, let's go in and have a drink. I could use one. Not to mention a sit-down.'

Particularly a sit-down. Delayed shock had suddenly turned her insides to water, and made her start to tremble.

Rider's arm securely round her, they went into Yesterday at Pascal's, with its ornate glass doors and looped velvet curtains.

By the time they were met and greeted with great cordiality by the suave and elegant proprietor in person, Rider was once more in command. As soon as they'd been shown to one of the private booths, he asked for a couple of brandies to be sent over, adding, 'We had a spot of trouble and my car's by the kerb, its keys left in the ignition; can someone move it?'

'Certainly, sir.' The *maître d'* hastened away to do his bidding.

'Knowing New York, it's probably been stolen by now,' Dita tried to joke.

'A car's easily replaced.' Reaching across the table, Rider took her hand, gripping the slim fingers hard. 'Unlike some things.'

Since they'd met for the second time, Rider hadn't said he loved her. He might *never* say he loved her. But tonight's events had proved that in some strange, tortuous way he cared, and cared deeply.

He released her hand as the brandies arrived.

By the time her glass was empty, the warming liquor had done its work and Dita was feeling almost herself again. The meal was very good, but she ate mechanically, sunk deep in thought. It had been a strange, tumultuous day, she reflected. The assault, or rather its aftermath, had, like holding up a mirror, added yet another dimension to her relationship with Rider.

But if he really cared for her, how did Julie Dawn fit into his life?

'Should I be jealous?' Rider's question broke into her abstraction.

'What?' she asked blankly.

'You've been staring over my head for a good five minutes.'

'Oh...' Making an effort to gather her woolly wits, Dita focused on the spot indicated and discovered she'd been gazing unseeingly at a black and white picture of a sexy, smouldering Rudolph Valentino, as the Sheikh.

Though Valentino wasn't her type at all, she answered with a grin, 'Well, he was rather gorgeous. All flashing eyes and Latin charm.'

Rider's grimace made her elaborate mischievously, 'One of my girlish fantasies was to be seized by a handsome sheikh who'd throw me over his saddle and gallop off into the desert with me.'

'Suppose when you'd reached his tent you'd discovered he suffered from halitosis and wasn't too particular about personal hygiene?'

'Oh, I never reached his *tent*,' she said in a shocked voice. 'When we moved to the States we had a Quaker housekeeper. Lally...as a young child I couldn't say Alice...had very strict morals. She not only expected my actions to be full of propriety, but my thoughts to be pure as driven snow.

'She'd have had a blue fit if she'd even suspected about my rides through the desert... No, it was all very innocent. And, to be truthful, Valentino doesn't turn me on.'

'Then I've no need to be jealous,' Rider said.

'Not really.' Her answer was equally flippant. 'Oh...' A sip from her cup told Dita she'd allowed her coffee to get cold.

Rider signalled the waiter, and when they'd been served with a fresh tray commented lightly, 'Perhaps everyone should have a guardian angel to take care of their morals.'

She shot him a quick glance from beneath long lashes.

His grey eyes narrowed dangerously. 'Go on, say it.'

'I wasn't going to say anything.'

'Oh, yes, you were. Something along the lines of, "It's a pity *you* didn't."'

He'd read her mind so accurately that she flushed.

The band struck up with 'Lady be Good', and several couples took to the small square of highly polished floor.

'And as a matter of fact, I *did*,' he went on, having observed her heightened colour with grim satisfaction. 'My grandmother, bless her heart, was of the same ilk as your Lally.'

'So what happened?' Dita refused to be browbeaten. 'How did you manage to earn your playboy reputation?'

'In spite of everything the gossip columnists conjectured or dreamt up, I did very little. A youthful fling then a couple of semi-serious relationships hardly constitutes being a rake. Of course I had the doubtful pleasure of someone else's reputation brushing off on me...' He stopped speaking abruptly.

After a moment, the sudden flare of bitterness under control, he went on, 'The only way I could have avoided the kind of unwarranted publicity I got was to have become a hermit. I just had to speak to a woman to be bedding her. Talk about a super-stud! The amount of different women I was supposed to be keeping happy would have made Casanova envious... Whereas one woman is all I've ever needed.'

'Then I've no need to be jealous.' She echoed his earlier words.

'Not really.' Rider echoed hers.

If only that were true.

With a sudden impetuous desire to *know*, she took off at a tangent. 'I phoned Kate today.'

'Oh?' He displayed only polite interest.

'You have been in touch with her since we got back?' She made it a question.

'Yes.'

'You didn't tell me.'

'Perhaps I didn't want you to know.'

She tried a new approach. 'I was expecting us to have a heart-to-heart. Kate had admitted to feeling guilty about something; something that clearly concerned our break-up. I thought she was going to tell me what it was.'

'Why didn't she tell you after our wedding lunch?'

'She presumed I knew. There was no time then to talk, to clear the air, so she suggested we get in touch later...

'When she didn't ring I decided to call her. While I was looking for the Washington number in the phone pad I came across Julie Dawn's number and address.' Even in her own ears it sounded like an accusation.

'And what does that make me guilty of?'

'As I don't know when you made the entry, nothing. It might have dated from the time Kate was going to tell me about.'

'*Was* going to?' he asked blandly.

'You know very well she didn't. Because it would have helped to prove your guilt, you stopped her.' Recklessly she flung the accusation at him, infuriated by his stone-walling tactics. 'And don't bother to deny it,' she added for good measure.

'I wasn't going to deny it. But I don't know why you need extra proof. As far as you're concerned my guilt has never been in doubt.' He was quietly, *furiously* angry.

'But you *admitted* it,' she cried. 'If you weren't Julie Dawn's lover, if her baby wasn't yours, *why* did you admit it? If you'd only tell me that...'

'If I'd only tell you that,' he mimicked her savagely, 'you *might* trust me. What a marvellous incentive...' With a kind of raging calm he went on, 'Only, you see, I don't care a damn for your trust. Trust that has a price tag, that has to be bought, isn't worthy of the name. I need you to love me and——'

'I *do* love you,' she broke in desperately.

He laughed contemptuously. 'You can keep your so-called love. As far as I'm concerned love and trust are indivisible, they go hand in hand, make up one wonderful, shining, spiritual whole.

'As I told you once before, if I can't have that, I'll settle for a purely physical relationship to gratify my obsession. Only don't try to dress it up with the name of love.'

Her heart rent and bleeding, her face as white as the linen tablecloth, her green eyes clouded with pain, Dita sat staring at him.

Earlier she'd told herself he *cared*. But obviously she'd been mistaken. His reaction had simply been confirming the strength of the obsession he'd more than once admitted to.

For a moment he sat quite still, his jaw clenched, then, his face wiped clean of expression, as if he'd closed a curtain on the little scene that had just taken place, he asked politely, 'Would you like to dance?'

After an energetic Charleston, the band had drifted into a smoochy Jerome Kern number.

The last thing she wanted right now was the empty mockery of being held close in his arms. Fighting back tears, she shook her head. 'I couldn't venture on the dance-floor in these stockings.'

'Have they got ladders?'

She laughed shakily. 'I wouldn't call them ladders, they're more like marble staircases.' Then, knowing she couldn't sit here a moment longer, she cleared her throat and said, 'If you don't mind, I'd like to go home.'

He rose to his feet. 'Of course. It's been quite a night.'

Beneath his light remark she could sense a white-hot lava flow of bitterness and anger that made her afraid.

CHAPTER TEN

WHEN they reached the penthouse, with his customary unstudied courtesy Rider helped Dita off with her coat. His lean fingers accidentally brushed against her breast and she flinched.

His lips twisted at the betraying movement and, the bones of his face locked tight in anger, he deliberately put his hand over the soft curve, fingers moving lightly, erotically across the firming nipple.

Dita stood quite still, refusing to protest or back away though his touch burnt into her like a brand, and stared fixedly at the knot in his blue and grey striped tie.

With soft violence he said, 'I don't expect *trust*, but is a little physical contact too much to ask?'

'Yes, it is,' she fought back. 'I don't want you to touch me. I'm not in the mood.'

'Now isn't that too bad?' With a swift movement she was totally unprepared for, he swung her up into his arms. 'Because, you see, I *am* in the mood, and I intend to touch and taste every little bit of you. Though you may *say* you don't want my touch, your body will respond gladly, and, having no liking for rape, I want a receptive woman.'

Rattled, hating the thought of being aroused against her will, she took refuge in anger. 'Well, you won't get one,' she retorted, with more conviction than she felt. And, knowing how her very bones seemed to melt when he merely looked at her, she added desperately, 'I mean it when I say I don't want you to touch me.'

'Perhaps if you close your eyes and pretend I'm a sheikh,' he suggested mockingly. 'Imagine I'm galloping off with you into the desert, intending to ravish you when we reach my tent. That might be exciting enough to make you change your mind.'

Ignoring his taunts, she said bitterly, 'If you're in the mood, why don't you go to Julie Dawn? I don't want to be used.'

'*Used* ... Is that how you see it?'

'Yes, it is.'

He laughed harshly, hostility implicit in his glance. 'Well, if making love to you is *using* you, then you certainly will be used, and used thoroughly.'

'Making love to me?' she choked. 'That's a euphemism if you like! At its best it's just lust, cheap passion.' Instantly she regretted her contemptuous words, knowing he'd punish her for them.

'Not cheap,' he flashed back, as he strode through into the bedroom. 'I could have bought myself a live-in whore at a great deal less expense.'

She flinched at his brutal choice of phrasing.

Laying her on the bed, he slipped off her shoes before switching on the bedside lamp to bathe her in a pool of light. She tried to struggle up but, leaning over her, he pulled her elbows forward until she flopped down again, his fingers sliding up her arms to imprison her there.

When she stayed still he sat on the edge of the mattress and began to stroke her lightly, but with intentional insolence. His hands were strong and well-shaped, his wrists sinewy and powerful, with a sprinkling of golden hair disappearing into the cuffs of his blue silk shirt.

Despite all her efforts, that touch, warm and possessive through the thin lilac georgette of her dress, almost immediately set up a spiralling coil of exquisite craving, a flood of wild hunger and excitement.

Knowing it was no use attempting to fight him, she remained motionless, as if some invisible force held her transfixed, trying to use mind over matter and quell her body's response. But it was like trying to prevent a finely tuned piano making music when a master ran his fingers over the keys.

She shivered as his hand lazily circled her abdomen and the moist warmth of his breath stimulated nipples already clearly visible through the clinging material.

For a moment he played with her long string of beads, tightening them lightly around her throat until her eyes widened with shock and disbelief.

His laugh was a soft, satisfied sound. 'There's no need to look so scared; I don't intend to strangle you,' he assured her, before slipping them over her head and tossing them aside. 'I have much more exciting plans for you.'

Her sense of outrage at his ruthless determination was like a scream in her mind. She knew what devils were driving him but, no matter how gentle, if he took her in anger, when tomorrow came he would be sorry. Only then it would be too late. Neither of them would ever forget.

When he bent to kiss her, she kept her lips pressed tightly together. Smiling a little, he ran his thumb sensuously across her mouth, easing her lips apart, brushing her pearly teeth.

Helplessly her mouth opened to him, but instead of taking advantage he moved to touch his lips to her temple, where a frantic pulse fluttered just beneath the skin.

Then slowly he began to undress her, savouring every inch of exposed flesh with a maddening thoroughness, his tongue seeking and unerringly finding each erogenous zone, one in particular making her gasp and shudder and causing her whole world to rock and shift focus.

Lifting his head, he asked softly, 'Did you enjoy that? Would you like me to do it again?'

Biting her lip, she refused to answer.

Satisfied, he said, 'When I kiss you there...or put my tongue there...your body reacts so beautifully.'

With careful fingers he unfastened her suspenders and began to ease down her stockings, following the delicate nylon with his lips.

All at once she heard the hiss of his breath. For a second or two he was quite still, looking at her badly grazed knees, the trickles of blood that had dried brown and crusty on her slim legs, then he muttered, 'Dear God, I must be mad after all you've gone through tonight...' In a flurry of movement he jumped to his feet, and a moment later the latch clicked decisively behind him.

Shivering, Dita sat up and stared at the closed door. Though her aroused body cried out for him, she could only be relieved that the reminder of the attack had brought him to his senses and caused that sudden change of heart.

Still shivering, she went into the bathroom and had a shower before cleaning her teeth and applying some salve to the grazes. Pulling on her nightdress, she switched off the lamp, crept beneath the covers and, wrapped in misery cold as any winding-sheet, lay in the semi-dark gazing at the ceiling.

There was no point in blaming Rider. It was her own stupidity that had totally spoilt what should have been a wonderful night... Though perhaps when he came to bed she could try to talk to him? Tell him she was sorry for what had happened, both in the restaurant and later, she hadn't meant them to quarrel. And it was the truth.

But, even if he accepted that, the damage was done.
Irreparable damage. She'd made it only too plain that
she still hadn't learnt to trust him. If she tried to tell
him any different now, he wouldn't believe her. And it
was certainly no time to blurt out her news. So what was
there to say *after* she'd said she was sorry?

The hours crept past on leaden feet, midnight, one-
thirty, two, and still Rider didn't come. There was no
sound from the living-room, and after another endless
hour of waiting Dita got out of bed, padded to the door,
and opened it. The lights still burnt, but the room was
empty. Was he so angry that he'd decided to sleep in the
guest room? Steeling herself, she went to look. But that
too was empty.

The luminous hand of the bedside clock showed five-
thirty in the morning before she finally fell into a troubled
sleep.

It was going up the hill for ten o'clock when she was
awakened by the telephone. Uneasy dreams still clinging
to her mind like an invisible but sticky spider's web that
refused to let go, she lifted the receiver and mumbled,
'Hello?'

'Mrs Barron, this is Rose, on the desk.' The new girl,
trying to sound efficient, only succeeded in sounding
scared, unsure of herself.

Struggling to free her trapped wits, Dita said, 'Yes,
Rose, what is it?'

'There's someone here who's asking to see Mr Barron.'

It would be... now what was his name...? Elmer
Winkler. 'I'm not sure where my husband is at the
moment,' Dita said. 'If I can't find him I'll come down
myself, so please ask the gentleman to wait.'

Feeling dazed and depressed, she replaced the receiver
and stumbled out of bed. The apartment *felt* empty. A
quick but comprehensive look proved it was, and showed

no sign of Rider having returned at all. Where had he
been all night? she wondered frantically, and tried not
to believe the answer that at once sprang to mind.

Well, if he *had* been with Julie Dawn it was her own
fault, she admitted bleakly, as she headed for the
bathroom. The kind of behaviour she'd indulged in was
practically guaranteed to drive him into another woman's
arms.

Some ten minutes later, showered and dressed in a
brown and beige checked skirt and a cream jumper, her
oval face pale, free of make-up, Dita ran a cursory comb
through her silky black hair and took the lift down.

It was Saturday morning, and many guests were still
in the breakfast-room, reading their papers while they
lingered over coffee. Apart from the staff there were no
more than a dozen people in the lobby, but a searching
glance failed to locate the youth she was looking for.

Dita was approaching the desk when Rose, blonde and
fresh-faced, spotted her and hurried forward to say,
'She's over there, Mrs Barron.'

'She?'

'I didn't get a chance to tell you...'

Stifling a sigh, Dita owned that it was her own fault
for jumping to conclusions. And if she hadn't been half-
asleep she would have asked for a name.

Having admitted as much, she added, 'But why didn't
you say a *lady*?'

Rose looked uncomfortable. 'Because she asked me
to say *someone*, and she refused to give a name.'

'Oh... Well, I'd better see if I can help.'

Dita made her way across the foyer to where a woman
was sitting in a deep chair by one of the huge fireplaces.
A hand clenched on the arm of the chair, a toe tapping,
suggested she was impatient, ill at ease.

She was well past her first youth but still beautiful, with glowing Titian hair and a complexion like thick cream. As well as a striking face and what was clearly a stunning figure, she had that indefinable quality that spelt glamour.

With a sudden startled flash of comprehension, Dita knew who she was, and froze.

At close quarters her face appeared older, and harder, showing a brittle confidence that Dita recognised with an odd compassion as a veneer to cover a continuous battle against life.

Hadn't she worn that same look herself? The look of someone who had been forced to take on the world single-handed and, unable to beat it, was struggling to hold it to a draw.

Suddenly eyes of a blue so deep as to be almost violet glanced her way and saw her.

Ignoring a craven urge to turn tail and run, she stood her ground with quiet dignity and introduced herself. 'Good morning, I'm Dita Barron. I understand you wanted to speak to my husband?'

Those amazing eyes registered surprise. 'So you're Rider's wife. You're not at all what I expected.'

'Really?' Dita reacted to the slight taunt. 'You're exactly what I expected.' She had the satisfaction of seeing the other woman momentarily at a disadvantage.

Almost immediately, however, the Titian-haired beauty rallied. Her shoulders squaring a little, as if bracing herself, she asked, 'Then you know who I am?'

'You're Ms Dawn, I take it.'

'So Rider's told you about me?'

Ignoring that, Dita said calmly, 'I'm afraid he isn't in at the moment. Would you like to leave a message? Or is there anything I can do for you?'

'I wouldn't be here except that I need to get in touch with him urgently. Do you know when he'll be back?'

'No, I'm afraid I don't.'

'Oh, hell!' For the first time Julie Dawn gave way to agitation. 'When I saw him yesterday afternoon he gave me a cheque to pay for Tasmin's operation...'

Dita thought of Rider's phone call, heard him saying '...something important's cropped up, and I won't have time to get home...'

'...but there's been a sudden change of plan,' the older woman was going on, 'and the hospital want to fly her to a specialist, one of the foremost men in his field, who's on a short visit to L.A.'

As if fearful about Dita's reactions, she rushed on with something akin to desperation, the words spilling out, 'Perhaps I'd better try to explain more fully. With the kind of terminal sarcoma condition Tasmin has, up until now normal surgery hasn't been able to offer much more than a thirty per cent chance of success.

'But there's recently been a break-through. A Swiss, a Dr Levesque, has been trying out a brand-new kind of surgery involving genetic engineering. Though it's still largely experimental it's so far given a seventy per cent success-rate.

'He has to return to Europe on Monday, but he's agreed to operate on Tasmin, if she can go now. Today. It's going to cost a great deal more money, but it means her chances are more than doubled. If only I could *see* Rider and explain...'

'Well, I'm sure you can go ahead and make the arrangements,' Dita said without hesitation. 'In fact, get in touch with the hospital right now.' As the other woman glanced around for the public phones, she suggested, 'Why don't you ring from the desk?'

When the brief call had been made and Julie Dawn came back, Dita added reassuringly, 'As soon as I can find Rider I'll ask him to come and see you...'

'Thank you.' Just for a moment the careful composure cracked, and tears swam in the violet eyes. Then, collecting herself, the dancer asked slowly, 'Don't you resent your husband spending money on a child that isn't yours?'

Dita shook her head. 'I don't even resent him spending money on a child that isn't his.'

'You sound very sure of that.'

Rider had said with certainty that the baby wasn't his and he hadn't just been denying responsibility, but the whole relationship. And suddenly she *knew* it was the truth.

He was human, with his share of faults, but he didn't lie. Only people who were weak, or selfish, or afraid, needed to lie to protect themselves. Rider was none of those things. He was an unselfish, compassionate man, with a clear perception of right and wrong and a strong sense of duty.

'I am sure,' she said serenely.

'Can I ask what makes you so certain?'

'He told me so.'

'Most women would take a lot more convincing than that.'

'I trust him.'

'That kind of trust doesn't come easy.'

Dita smiled crookedly. 'You can say that again.'

As the older woman turned to leave, Dita said quickly, 'I hope everything goes well and the operation is successful.'

Julie smiled, a warm and genuine smile. 'Thank you... You're very kind.' It wasn't just a trite phrase.

When Dita reached the penthouse, to her surprise and relief Rider was back, standing by the window looking out over the park, tension in the set of his head and shoulders.

He swung round at her entrance, and she caught an expression of relief that was swiftly masked. Huskily, he said, 'I wondered where you'd got to.'

'You didn't come through the lobby?'

'No.'

'That's where I was.'

There was a pause while they stared at each other. He looked tired and drawn, Dita thought. His thick blond hair was slightly rumpled, golden stubble adorned his chin, and he still had on the clothes he'd worn the previous night.

Grey eyes cool and guarded now, he asked, 'Don't you want to know where I've been?'

'Not unless you want to tell me.'

'What if I admit to having come straight from Julie Dawn's bed?'

'I wouldn't believe you.'

'My, my, you are doing well! A bit more practice and you'll have me convinced you trust me!'

Ignoring the hated mockery, she lassoed her courage and, at the risk of being repulsed, said steadily, 'I'm sorry about last night; if you had gone to Julie Dawn I couldn't have blamed you, and I'm sorry we quarrelled in the restaurant.'

His face softening a little, he suggested, 'Suppose we put it down to the shock of what happened earlier?'

Shaking her head, she demurred, 'Don't let's make excuses or gloss over things. It was due to my lack of trust.'

'But when I told you I'd come straight from Julie's bed you refused to believe me.'

Levelly, she admitted, 'I wouldn't believe you because I've just been talking to Ms Dawn . . .'

'Ah . . . So that's what you were doing in the lobby.'

'She wants to speak to you urgently.'

'Indeed?' His lips twisted. 'Tell me, what did you think of your red-headed rival?'

Refusing to rise to the bait, Dita answered, 'I felt sorry for her.'

Genuinely surprised, he stated, 'There are times you still amaze me! You've got a spirit of pure steel and a heart as soft as a marshmallow.' His mouth taking on a wry slant, he added caustically, 'Didn't you find Ms Dawn too hard-boiled to warrant much sympathy?'

'On the surface, maybe. But if that's what you really believe, why are you helping her?'

'Don't you think I might have an obligation?'

Dita shook her head. 'No. I think you're doing it out of the goodness of your heart.'

For a moment he looked taken aback, then, eyes narrowing to gleaming grey slits, he demanded, 'Exactly what did she have to say?'

'Very little except that you'd given her a cheque to pay for her daughter's operation.'

'There must have been more.'

Dita shrugged. 'If you can't take my word, ask her.' After a moment she pressed, 'You will call and see her as soon as possible, won't you?'

'What can be so urgent?'

'The hospital want to fly her daughter to L.A. There's a specialist there who can offer the child a much better chance of recovery. But it has to be *now*. I'll leave it with her to explain and give you the details. Incidentally,' Dita continued hardily, 'with time being so short I told her to go ahead, on your behalf.'

Raising his eyebrows, he said, 'Did you, now?'

'Well, I was sure you'd want her to.'

His jaw tightened a little. 'May I ask on what grounds?'

Dita met his eyes squarely, handsome eyes with clear dark grey irises surrounded by even darker rings. 'Humanitarian.'

'Perhaps I should point out that I'm no soft touch.'

Deciding that it might be as well to placate the male ego, Dita agreed, 'I know that, and I'm sure she does. Beneath that hard exterior you mentioned she was worried sick you might refuse.'

'Then as soon as I've shaved and changed I'll go and put her mind at rest.' His face sardonic, he added, 'But before I do, tell me one thing; what made you go down to see her? Were you planning a confrontation?'

'No,' Dita said shortly. 'I mistakenly thought the someone who wanted to see you was Elmer Winkler.'

'Ah.'

'I hope he comes. He needs help before he does something else stupid and lands in real trouble.'

'He's already been.'

Her green eyes on Rider's face, Dita waited.

'When I came back first thing this morning I met him on the doorstep. We had a long talk over breakfast and I discovered that he's fascinated by computers, so on Monday he's starting training with RMB Electronics. Until he can stand on his own two feet, I've arranged for him to have bed and board here.'

'That's marvellous,' Dita said.

Rider shrugged non-committally. 'We'll see how things work out. At least he has a chance.'

He turned and went into the bedroom. A few seconds afterwards she heard the bathroom door close behind him and the shower start to run.

Some twenty-five minutes later, dressed with casual elegance, his chin smooth, his hair neatly combed but still damp, he left with just a mocking salute.

Dita sighed. She'd hoped that once they'd talked, got back on some kind of normal footing, the situation would improve. But their brief meeting hadn't been comfortable, nor had it solved anything. Though civil, they had been like opponents in a fencing match, *en garde*, warily circling each other.

She ate her lunch alone, and by mid-afternoon there was still no sign of Rider. Steadfastly refusing to allow the smallest pricks of jealousy, she'd just decided to go down to the pool when there was a tap at the door.

Wondering why he wasn't using his key, she hurried to open it, a smile on her lips. To her surprise it was a well-dressed but harassed-looking Kate who stood there.

'Well, hello! Come on in,' Dita invited, and thought how odd it was that when they'd been talking on the phone the other woman hadn't mentioned she would be in Manhattan the next day.

Kate hesitated, then asked in a low voice, 'Is Rider home?'

'No, I'm afraid he isn't.'

Breathing what sounded remarkably like a sigh of relief, Kate followed Dita through the hall and into the living-room.

'Would you like a cup of tea or coffee?' It felt strange to be playing hostess.

'I'd love a coffee.' Taking off her cashmere coat, Kate tossed it negligently over a chair. 'But let's have it in the kitchen. It's somehow more homely.'

'Are you staying in town?' Dita asked as she spooned coffee into the percolator.

'Just for the weekend.' Kate sat down at the stripped pine table in the large, airy kitchen. 'Dan's waiting for me at the Waldorf. I told him I fancied a trip to New York, so we're seeing a show tonight and being last-minute guests at a charity concert tomorrow, before heading back to Washington, DC...'

Thinking she'd heard a door close, Dita cocked an ear. When there was no further sound, realising she'd been mistaken, she gave her full attention to the other woman, who was smoothing the pleated skirt of her cherry-coloured Charivari dress with restless fingers.

'I just *had* to come,' Kate burst out suddenly. 'Rider won't be pleased—he told me to keep out of it and he's not a man I would normally care to cross—but I want everything to be right between you. I can't let you go on worrying about Julie Dawn.'

Dita smiled and said gently, 'I'm no longer worrying about Julie Dawn. I've wrung the necks of all my doubts and started to do what I should have done from the start—trust Rider.'

'Thank God... That was what he wanted more than anything. He said if you loved him enough you'd trust him. I told him in my humble opinion to expect that kind of blind trust was asking too much of any woman.

'You see, when we got the wedding invitation, I thought he must have told you everything. It came as a complete surprise when he rang up after New Year and warned me bluntly to keep my mouth shut.

'I tried to convince him it wasn't fair to leave you in the dark, but after everything that had happened he was too pigheaded to let me tell you. All he would say was, "She has to *trust* me, otherwise it's no use."'

Dita sighed. 'When he told me Julie Dawn's baby wasn't his, I *wanted* to trust him, I *tried* to trust him, but I always came back to the fact that he'd *admitted* everything.

'It's only now that I've come to accept and believe that if he told me I was the only woman in his life, then I was, he wouldn't lie to me... I don't know why he

confessed to something that wasn't true, especially to
the Press, but he must have had a very good reason.'

'Oh, he had. You see, he was...'

Dita shook her head. 'Don't say anything. Rider didn't
want you to, and there's no need. Really there isn't. One
of these days when he believes I trust him, he might tell
me himself.'

'What if he doesn't?' Kate looked at her with worried
blue eyes.

'If he doesn't, he doesn't,' Dita said simply. 'I can
live with that.'

'But I feel so *guilty*.'

'Don't feel guilty. It's all right, honestly it is.'

After some hesitation, Kate said, 'Well, in that case
I'll take myself off before Rider gets home.'

Dita gave the other woman a swift hug. 'Thanks for
coming. I really do appreciate it! And don't worry. Now
I no longer have any doubts, if it's the last thing I do
I'll *make* things work, *make* Rider love me.'

Kate looked surprised. 'You're joking, surely? He's
always loved you.'

He had once, but Kate didn't know the half of it, Dita
thought, as she let the other woman out and watched
her petite figure hurry towards the lift.

Sadly she admitted that, despite her brave words, she
was dreadfully afraid she had lost Rider's love forever.

And perhaps she deserved to, having been wrong about
so many things. She'd convinced herself that Rider had
prevented his stepmother helping to prove his guilt, but
clearly Kate had been trying to prove not his guilt but
his *innocence*. An innocence Dita now believed in totally.

If it hadn't been for last night's quarrel, she thought
sadly, it could have been a wonderful evening...

No...no! It was time she stopped fooling herself. High time she threw aside the rose-coloured glasses that saved her from having to look at reality, and faced the truth.

Just loving Rider hadn't been sufficient. It was no use trying to gloss over the more than evident cracks in their relationship. It was clear now that if their marriage was to survive they needed a new, stronger foundation to build on. If he didn't love her, then a basis of caring and respect, of total honesty and trust, would surely be enough. She was willing to try, to sweep the skeletons out of the cupboards and make a new start...

But would *he* be?

All Rider had owned to was an obsession. Only he knew whether his true feelings were deep enough to last a lifetime. And she had to have the answer to that question before she told him her news. Otherwise she would never know for certain whether it was *that* which had influenced him.

Shivering, she faced the fact that his answer might be no. If he thought they had no future together, what would she do then?

Squaring her shoulders, she told herself she would do what many other women had to do—she would make a new life for herself and her child. She would leave Rider free to find happiness with some other woman. But before she could make any decision she had to talk to him, to come to a clear understanding.

As though her thoughts had conjured him up, there he was, standing in the doorway, watching her. His raw-boned face wore a strange expression that she was unable to decipher, a look that hinted at some powerful emotion being held in check.

'Oh, you're back!' she exclaimed inanely. 'I didn't hear you come in... Did you see Ms Dawn?'

'I did. Everything's fixed.' A muscle jumped in his cheek. 'I also saw Kate.'

'Oh...' Was the emotion anger? 'Did you speak to her?' Dita asked carefully.

Grey eyes glittered. 'No, I listened. You could say eavesdropped...'

So she *had* heard a door closing...

'Walking in to hear that conversation rocked me back on my heels, yet it only served to confirm what Julie had already told me.' As though the words were torn from him, he asked raggedly, 'Do you really trust me, Perdita?'

'Yes,' she answered simply, then, in a cry of anguish, 'If only I had done from the start it would have saved so much heartache.'

'Possibly, given our backgrounds and differences in lifestyles, the heartache was inevitable... At least that's what I told myself last night while I walked the streets.'

Dita shuddered. Rider must have been out of his mind. Even for a tough, well-built man, walking the streets of Manhattan in the middle of the night was a singularly risky business.

After a moment he went on, 'I knew it was too late, we were at the end of the road. We couldn't go on as we had been doing...'

'But it's not too late...' she protested with desperate eagerness. 'We could start again on a different footing, couldn't we?'

'I don't know,' he admitted heavily. 'I've made so many mistakes...'

Gripped by an icy panic, she could only stare at him, her hands clenched until the nails bit into her palms.

After a moment, he went on, 'Before any decision is reached, we need to talk.'

'Yes... Oh, yes...' She felt a sudden longing to be back in the Catskills, the two of them huddled by the glowing range in the cabin, or sitting by the fire at Rider's Keep.

They hadn't gone to the Keep since their marriage. It had often been on the tip of her tongue to suggest it, but somehow she never had. Now, as though the old house had magic powers, it was suddenly important to go there, to return to the place where it had all begun.

Taking a deep breath, she asked steadily, 'Were you thinking of eating out tonight?'

Slowly, he shook his head. 'I wasn't... But if you'd like to?'

'Yes, please.'

An expression that could have been disappointment was swiftly masked. 'Have you somewhere special in mind?'

She nodded. 'Yes, I have, very special.'

A polite stranger now, he said, 'If it's likely to be crowded it might be a good idea to phone up and book a table.'

'I don't think it's likely to be crowded, but it might be a good idea to give Mrs Merriton a ring.'

When he said nothing, she added anxiously, 'You don't *mind* a weekend at the Keep, do you? Only it's ages since I've been, and I was thinking how nice it would be to go.'

'No, I don't mind.' He studied her keenly. 'I would have suggested it myself, but I thought it might hold some not too pleasant memories for you.'

'Nothing of the kind,' she denied. 'It's always seemed like a haven.' Pressing her advantage, she suggested, 'Shall I put a few things into a case while you phone?'

He nodded his agreement. 'Very well, Perdita.'

CHAPTER ELEVEN

IN LESS than half an hour they were making their way through the wintry dusk. It had been a bitterly cold day but clear, and, though it was now clouding over, the road surfaces were dry, conditions good.

Traffic proved to be relatively light, and they were soon heading out of town. Rider drove in silence, his face set in lines that discouraged if not actually forbade conversation.

Sighing, Dita looked out of the window and thought about her first trip to the Keep, just over a year ago. A lot had happened since then. So much to be thankful for. A great deal that still needed to be faced, with their marriage, their future, hanging in the balance...

By the time they reached the southern rim of the mountains, clouds were unravelling themselves across the night sky and dangling in grey wisps that threatened snow.

When they reached the lamplit, welcoming house, Mrs Merriton was in the hall to greet them warmly. Giving Dita one of her rare smiles, she said, 'It's nice to have you back.'

Dita returned the smile. 'It's nice to be back. How are you keeping?'

'I used to get a bit lonely until Mr Rider suggested I have Sean to keep me company, but now I'm fine.'

Lifting startled eyes, Dita queried, 'Sean? Is he a cat?'

'Cat?' the housekeeper exclaimed. 'He certainly is not. Sean,' she raised her voice, 'come and meet Mr and Mrs Barron.'

174

From out of the kitchen lumbered the biggest Irish wolfhound Dita had ever seen. Grey and hairy, with feet the size of saucers, he looked like a child's pony.

He came quietly, docilely, a gentle giant, but his brown eyes were watchful, and Dita, who had no fear of animals, viewed him with respect and waited to be introduced before she offered to stroke that shaggy head.

'Sean's an absolute lamb, and very obedient,' Mrs Merriton enthused. 'He only barks if I tell him to, and he's as good as gold in the house...' She pulled herself up. 'Well, now, Mr Rider said you'd want to eat in front of the living-room fire...Dinner's all ready to serve, and I dare say you're starving.'

While Rider carried their overnight case upstairs, Dita settled herself by the hearth and watched the leaping flames reflected in the bow-fronted sideboard. By the bookshelves a single standard lamp provided a soft pool of radiance, and the tick-tock of the grandfather clock was as familiar as an old friend. Yet the previous sense of relaxed comfort was missing; all she could feel was her own growing tension.

When Rider joined her, she waited for him to speak, but he said nothing, apparently deep in thought.

Perhaps it was as well to leave the talking until later, Dita decided, as she studied his half-averted face, and by keeping the most stringent hold on herself managed to wait with a veneer of calm until a few minutes later Mrs Merriton brought in the dinner trolley.

Apart from drawing Rider's attention to the snow-flakes starting to drift against the diamond-leaded panes, Dita made no attempt at conversation and they ate in silence.

As soon as the housekeeper came in to wheel away the remnants of the meal, Dita went to sit by the hearth.

Rider, who seemed to have been waiting for her to move, followed and dropped into a low chair opposite.

There was a long pause while they both stared into the fire. Her heart hammering against her ribs, Dita waited for him to make the first move.

His face set, as though he was keeping a tight hold on his emotions, he began abruptly, 'Kate was right...I haven't been fair to you. I should have told you the whole truth straight away rather than expecting blind trust. If I had done, things might have been very different...'

A log slipped and sent up a shower of bright sparks. He pushed it into place with the toe of his shoe before resuming his seat and continuing, 'My father has always had a...shall I be charitable and say a *penchant* for women? My mother realised that almost as soon as they were married, and though she spent the next twenty years following him around she never succeeded in keeping him on the straight and narrow for more than a few weeks at a time.'

Dita cringed at the bitterness in Rider's voice, but, guessing it was doing him good to talk, to get it out of his system, she urged, 'Go on.'

'*His* reputation for being a playboy was well earned—whereas mine was reflected glory, so to speak—though as he'd begun to climb the ladder, and his political career took off, he'd become of necessity, much more discreet in his dealings with women.

'When, after my mother's death, he met and married Kate, I hoped for her sake he'd finally decided to settle down. And for a while it seemed as if he had. Then, just when I thought his affairs were a thing of the past, Julie Dawn got her hooks into him...'

Her hands clasped tightly together, Dita made a small sound like a sigh. Now she'd been told, the pieces fell into place like a jigsaw puzzle.

'There's not much doubt he was set up,' Rider went on. 'Add together a not so young dancer who was losing both her agility and her looks and was on a slippery downward slope, and an unscrupulous boyfriend, and you have a lethal combination.

'They hoped to make a killing, and might well have succeeded if they hadn't been a shade too greedy and miscalculated. But, though my father's a wealthy man, most of his money is tied up in property and such like.

'He was having so much difficulty trying to raise the massive sum of cash Julie was demanding to keep his name out of the papers that Kate found out. Though he didn't deserve it, she promised to stand by him and help him find the money.

'However, Kate's a shrewd woman and it didn't take her long to realise that even if he paid up, once the gossip columnists had got their teeth into a juicy story they wouldn't easily let go. They'd keep on digging until they unearthed something damning.

'Julie had hinted that the man involved was a wealthy banker, which had been enough to put them on the scent. Then they came up with those blasted signatures...'

'But they'd picked the wrong Rider Barron...' Dita breathed.

'Exactly. That fact gave Kate her idea... You see, once mud starts to fly in the political arena it sticks to both guilty and innocent alike. Not only her husband, but her son, Richard, who was representing one of the more puritanical States, was in danger of having his career if not ruined, then certainly blighted. Kate adores her son and she's nothing if not loyal, so she wanted to save them both.

'All this blew up the night of that damned party. I was on my way to the airport the following morning when Kate spoke to me on the car phone. She begged for help, saying that if *I* confessed to being the man involved it would take the wind out of Julie Dawn's sails and scotch the plot once and for all.

'She pointed out that what wouldn't hurt *me* could destroy my father and stepbrother, and as I'd never taken any notice of adverse publicity and had nothing to lose...

'But for the first time in my life I *had* something to lose, and I told her so in no uncertain terms.

'When she realised how strongly I felt about you she was ready to forget the whole thing, but for her sake and for Richard's I agreed to go ahead. As far as my father was concerned I felt nothing but contempt for him and I'd have seen him burn in hell without lifting a finger.'

Shocked, Dita cried, 'You don't mean that.'

'Give me one good reason why I should feel any other way. He spoilt my mother's life through his inability to be faithful, and he was more than ready to abandon me because a baby didn't fit in with his lifestyle.' Though Rider spoke without undue heat, anger was there, and the deep-rooted pain of rejection.

Dita looked at him with a combination of sadness and compassion. 'I wish you weren't so bitter...'

Ignoring the barely audible words, he went on, 'Knowing it was no use trying to speak to you at the office, Kate promised she would call and see you that evening and explain what was happening in case you happened to read it in any of the papers.'

'But that was the evening I went out with Stephen...'

'Yes... Apparently she hung about for ages before deciding to leave it until next morning. Then next morning fate took a hand. On her way to your apartment she was involved in an accident; it was only slight but it delayed her for over an hour. She must have just missed you.'

'If only I'd waited,' Dita whispered.

'To give Kate her due, she was distraught when she realised you'd vanished. She rang me in San Francisco and I walked out of the conference and got on the next plane.' He was speaking in a flat, expressionless voice that told more clearly than any histrionics how deep his feelings went.

'As soon as I arrived back I began to look for you, but no one had the faintest idea where you'd gone. I hired a firm of detectives who scoured New York for months. When they couldn't find any trace of you, I think I went a little mad...'

Feeling as though bands of steel were constricting her heart, Dita knew that at least some of Rider's bitterness could be directed at her legitimately. Hadn't he once said, "I staked everything on you trusting me"?

Through dry lips she asked, 'So what happened between you and Julie Dawn?'

'My unexpected admission spiked her guns. At first she tried to get money out of me by declaring the baby was my father's, but when I made it clear I'd check on times and insist on a blood test she admitted it was her boyfriend's. It was discovering she was pregnant that had sparked off the whole thing.

'When her boyfriend found that no money would be forthcoming, he tried to persuade her to have an abortion. She flatly refused, and he walked out on her.

'She asked me for help and, because I admired her for keeping the baby, I agreed to support her until the child was born and she could begin work again.

'But it turned out to be not so simple. Her little girl was delicate from the start, and *she* was unable to dance any more, so her career was over.

'A few months ago she met a decent man who wanted to marry her, and it looked as if things were going to

improve, but then the child's illness was diagnosed...
Her husband would willingly have paid for the operation, but he wasn't in a position to, so once again she
asked me for help... The rest you know.'

Dita felt absurdly proud. Rider was a wonderful
person, generous and compassionate. How many men
in the same situation would have acted as he had?

After a brief silence he added, 'You and I have had
our lives almost ruined, and Kate, who was only trying
to help those she loved, has suffered the tortures of the
damned, while my father, whose fault it all was, has got
off scot-free. Can you wonder I'm bitter?'

'No,' she admitted. 'But I wish you'd put the past
behind you. Your father was weak rather than anything
else, and bitterness is corrosive. It doesn't necessarily
hurt the person it's directed at, but it can blight and
destroy the person who *feels* it... Please, Rider, can't
you forgive him?'

'Can *you*?'

'Yes,' she answered unhesitatingly. 'The thing I'm
finding most difficult is learning to forgive myself. *I'm*
the one who must bear the brunt of the blame...' When
Rider would have protested, she shook her head. 'It
wasn't your father who caused our break-up, it was my
lack of trust.'

Once again he would have interrupted, but she hurried
on, 'If you can't forgive your father you may never be
able to forgive *me*.' Fear churning in her stomach and
roughening her breathing, she went on doggedly, 'But I
have to tell you everything, the whole truth...'

Seeing her desperation, he froze. 'What else is there
to tell me, Perdita?' Suddenly he was a stranger, stern,
steely-eyed, with the face of judgement and a set jaw.

She'd thought she was prepared, but now the moment
had come she felt miserably afraid. If only he'd reach

out and take her hand, sit her on his knee, show a softer side or give some indication that he cared.

'Rider, I . . . I don't really know how you feel about me . . .' They were the wrong words, not at all what she'd intended to say.

Sounding curt, he remarked, 'I doubt if you've ever known, Perdita. But you only have to ask.'

She made a desperate bid for lightness. 'Somehow it seems much harder than that.'

When he simply looked at her, his face implacable, she let it go and steeled herself to carry on, only the flicker of her long, dark lashes, the tension in her slim shoulders betraying her fear that she might be destroying what she was trying so hard to save.

'When I told you I loved you it was the truth. It was also true that though I was fond of Stephen I never *loved* him.

'As soon as we were married I realised I'd made a dreadful mistake. I couldn't bear him to touch me. God knows I tried to hide it, to be a wife to him, but every time he came near me I froze.

'That's one of the reasons our honeymoon was a nightmare. He got more and more frustrated and impatient and I got upset and overwrought . . .'

She hesitated, then blurted out, 'I was pregnant and suffering from a morning sickness which seemed to last twenty-four hours a day and made me on edge and wretched.

'We quarrelled, and I felt terribly guilty. But at the same time I knew it was no use, I'd never be able to feel anything but warm friendship for him. And even that would be spoilt because he wanted so much more, so much I could never give——'

A dark flush lying across his hard cheekbones, Rider interrupted fiercely, 'But you've just told me you were pregnant. You were carrying his baby.'

Her oval face white as paper, her green eyes filled with apprehension, she shook her head. 'It wasn't his baby.'

Rider's expression was as bleak as the Arctic. Through clenched teeth he demanded, 'If the baby wasn't his, whose was it?'

Her pale lips framed the single word, though no sound came. 'Yours.'

His eyes darkened to charcoal as he absorbed the shock. Hoarsely he said, 'So it was *my* baby you lost?'

She nodded wordlessly, and waited for his reaction. This was the crunch. Everything depended on him accepting what she had to tell him, and understanding why she hadn't told him before. But he seemed stunned, incapable of speech or movement.

As the silence lengthened unbearably, she made a great effort to find her voice and take up her story again. 'When I tried to explain to Stephen how rotten I was feeling, he thought I was just making excuses . . . and perhaps subconsciously I was——'

'You mean to say he didn't *know* you were expecting?' Rider broke in urgently.

'Of course he knew. That was one of the reasons we got married.'

'Go on.' The two words fell into the silence like pebbles into an icy pond.

Dita swallowed hard. 'I'd only been in Georgia for a short time when I realised I was pregnant. At first I tried to keep it secret, but it isn't easy to hide morning sickness . . .

'Partly for my sake, and partly to save his mother's feelings, Stephen let her believe the baby was his. She was thrilled to bits, and began to go on about us getting married.

'Perhaps if she'd lived I'd have found the courage to tell her the truth. But as you know, she didn't, and her death proved to be a catalyst.

'His hotel chain offering accommodation to married employees was one of the reasons Stephen began to press me to marry him. The baby was one of the reasons I accepted. I was feeling ill and depressed, with no idea of how I was going to cope, and Stephen was kindness itself...'

'Until you were married,' Rider commented grimly.

'Don't blame him, it wasn't his fault,' Dita cried passionately, 'it was mine. He'd hoped for a warm, loving wife; all he got was a pasty-faced, frigid woman who cringed every time he went near her. No wonder he was upset and disappointed.

'When I couldn't stand that awful hotel, the pressure a moment longer, I told him I wanted to leave. He was angry, and when I insisted on going we had yet another furious quarrel.

'I should have had more sense than to let him drive, the mood he was in... It was a bitterly cold day with temperatures well below freezing. We were taking a bend much too fast when the car hit a patch of black ice and went out of control. We glanced off the Wilsons' pick-up truck and rolled down a steep, rocky hillside.

'It all happened so fast that at the time I didn't realise another vehicle was involved or anyone else had been hurt. It wasn't until weeks later that they told me what had happened. How the pick-up had also veered off the road and hit a tree...' She was forced to swallow past a painful lump in her throat before going on, 'And how

Paul, who hadn't had his seatbelt fastened, had been catapulted through the windscreen.

'I knew the accident had been my fault; if Stephen and I hadn't quarrelled, if I hadn't insisted on leaving the hotel, it would never have happened.

'Paul was only seven at the time, and his life was in ruins. I felt shattered all over again, torn apart by guilt...' Twin tears rolled down her cheeks.

Quietly, Rider said, 'While not accepting that any blame attached to you, I can quite understand why you were so anxious to help the Wilsons, to do everything you could for the child.'

Dita rubbed a hand over her eyes. 'At first I didn't want you to get involved, but soon just knowing you were helping them took some of the weight off my conscience. I was so *grateful*, but you were so prickly about it that I've never been able to thank you, to tell you how I felt.'

Looking uncomfortable, Rider said, 'I was a fool to create such a situation, but I was desperate to keep some hold over you, to make sure you didn't just walk out of my life again.'

Her eyes searched his face. 'I don't understand why, if you no longer loved me.'

His laugh held self-derision. 'At first I told myself it was because I wanted reparation for the pain you'd caused when you ran out on me. It was only later I admitted that you'd become an obsession.'

After a moment he sighed and said, 'But you were telling me about the accident. You say your car rolled down a hillside. Were you...?'

'We were trapped inside.' Her eyes full of darkness, she added, 'Because the tank had ruptured and there was gasoline everywhere it took the emergency services well over four hours to cut us out, and, as you know, Stephen, who had severe head injuries, never regained consciousness.'

Rider began, 'But you told me he died...' Then, with a dawning, horrified comprehension, 'You don't mean he was in a coma for more than three years?'

'Yes, he was. From the start the doctors told me there was virtually no hope, but I refused to believe them. Because I felt responsible, I couldn't *let* myself believe them.

'It was a long time before I finally accepted that to all intents and purposes Stephen had died in the accident.'

'God in heaven,' Rider muttered. 'It's a miracle they got you out of it alive.'

'I was conscious for most of the time, but trapped by the legs. I had internal injuries and was haemorrhaging badly. Before they could get me to hospital I'd lost the baby.'

His elbows on his spread knees, Rider dropped his head in his hands with a kind of muffled groan.

Dita stared at him and felt stricken. Because he usually hid his feelings so well, she wasn't used to witnessing such raw emotion. But now she was looking at a man who was being torn apart.

She got out of her chair and went down on her knees in front of him. 'I'm sorry; oh, darling, I'm sorry...' Then, in a cry from the heart, 'I can't bear to see you look like this.'

His arms closed around her and, his cheek pressed to hers, he held her so tightly that she thought her ribs might crack. '*I'm* the one who should be sorry. What you must have suffered...' A shudder ran through his big frame. 'How long were you in hospital?'

'Almost three months,' she tried to answer lightly. 'After a few weeks I was hobbling about, though at first

I had so many bandages I looked like a mobile mummy.'
She choked on a half-laugh, half-sob. 'Not a very apt
choice of words.'

Sounding anguished, he asked, 'Why didn't you tell
me all this before?'

'With so much tension on both sides I didn't know
how you'd take it. I was waiting, hoping we'd get on a
better footing before I told you the whole story.'

He groaned. 'I started out by almost believing I hated
you. It didn't take me long to realise that was far from
being the case.' His grip tightened. 'But, having got off
on the wrong foot, I made mistake after mistake and
the situation went from bad to worse. I let my own guilt
and frustration at the way things were turning out drive
me into becoming some kind of monster...'

She made a movement of denial, but he was going on,
'If I hadn't agreed to help Kate in the first place, or if
I'd had more sense the second time around... You were
saying that the whole thing's your fault, but in truth it's
mine...'

'Then we'll have to share the blame and forgive our-
selves and each other.'

He shook his head. 'I can't forgive myself. It's time
I let you go, got out of your life forever. I've brought
you nothing but unhappiness. The past will always be
there like a wall between us...'

Terrified, she clung to him. 'That's not true... It's
not! The past can only come between us if we let it.
What's done can't be undone but it can be——'

'Don't say forgotten,' he broke in savagely.

'No,' she admitted bravely, 'it can't be forgotten. But
it can be *accepted*. And once you've accepted it, it
ceases to hurt.'

'I find that hard to believe.' He let her go and lifted his head. His face looked grey and his eyes were filled with futile regrets and remorse.

'Believe it,' she urged. Lifting his hand, she held it to her cheek. 'Once I came to accept all that had happened, though I still felt sad at times, the worst of the pain vanished. I found I was free to put the past behind me and start again. But because we never talked openly, because neither knew what the other was thinking, it turned out to be a false start...'

Rider winced, and she saw his face tighten until the skin seemed to be stretched over the bones, but she continued steadily, 'You said we'd come to the end of the line, that we couldn't go on as we had been doing, and I agree...'

Taking a deep breath, she went on, 'I've told you all this because I want to stay with you, I want our marriage to last, and I hoped that once I'd been totally honest we could begin again, make a new start...

'Rider, you said if I wanted to know how you felt about me, all I had to do was ask. Well, I'm asking... If you feel anything at all, anything we can build on...'

'*If* I feel anything for you... Oh, Perdita...' The grey eyes glistened with tears.

It was heartbreaking to see a strong man so moved, and her own eyes filled with water. Stooping, he lifted her on to his knee and buried his face against her throat.

When he'd regained control, he raised his head and said deeply, 'You are the only woman I've ever loved. You're in my heart, my mind, my soul. You mean more to me than life itself. I don't deserve it, I know, but I want you to stay with me, to make me as happy as I intend to make you.'

She wound her arms tightly around his neck. 'I can't promise happiness all the way. There may be times when we're sad, but...'

'So long as we've got each other, nothing else matters. I don't care a damn if we can't have children...'

'So you've changed your mind about wanting a family?'

Watching him, she saw him swallow hard before he answered carefully, 'On reflection, I don't really think I'm cut out to be a father.'

'Now he tells me!'

He looked at her, obviously surprised by her words and tone.

She smiled at him brilliantly. 'Well, all I can say is, you'd better think again. I went to Dr Wiseman's clinic a couple of days ago and had lots of tests...'

'Are you telling me there's a possibility?' He failed totally to disguise the eagerness.

'Much better than that.' She ran her fingers through the thick hair curling in his nape, and drew his mouth to hers. Against his lips, she said, 'You've got until September to get into practice.'

'There's no mistake?'

'None. They tell me I'm fit as a fiddle and all set for a fine, healthy pregnancy.'

'My clever darling,' he cried exultantly.

She chuckled and, blushing enchantingly, pointed out, 'I did have a little help. Tell you what, if you're not quite sure about the role you played, let's have an early night and refresh your memory.'

His handsome face alight with laughter, he kissed her. 'My precious love, you're full of good ideas.'

*   *   *

Later that year, on the third of September, the New York gossip columnists had a field day.

Yesterday, Mr and Mrs Rider Barron became the proud parents of twins, a boy and a girl, born at Dr Wiseman's Park Avenue clinic. The babies and their mother are all doing well.

The wealthy banker, who held his wife's hand during the births, was obviously both relieved and delighted.

While the champagne flowed, I asked about names for the twins and was told that the boy will be called Rider Daniel, after his grandfather, and the little girl Perdita Kate.

I also learnt that the Barrons, who have been cited as New York's happiest couple, intend to fund a free gynaecological clinic on Lower East Side...

Accept 4 FREE Romances and 2 FREE gifts

FROM READER SERVICE

Here's an irresistible invitation from Mills & Boon. Please accept our offer of 4 FREE Romances, a CUDDLY TEDDY and a special MYSTERY GIFT! Then, if you choose, go on to enjoy 6 captivating Romances every month for just £1.80 each, postage and packing FREE. Plus our FREE Newsletter with author news, competitions and much more.

Send the coupon below to: Mills & Boon Reader Service, FREEPOST, PO Box 236, Croydon, Surrey CR9 9EL.

NO STAMP REQUIRED

Yes! Please rush me 4 FREE Romances and 2 FREE gifts! Please also reserve me a Reader Service subscription. If I decide to subscribe I can look forward to receiving 6 brand new Romances for just £10.80 each month, post and packing FREE. If I decide not to subscribe I shall write to you within 10 days - I can keep the free books and gifts whatever I choose. I may cancel or suspend my subscription at any time. I am over 18 years of age.

Ms/Mrs/Miss/Mr ＿＿＿＿＿＿＿＿＿＿＿＿＿＿＿＿＿＿＿＿＿ EP55R

Address ＿＿＿＿＿＿＿＿＿＿＿＿＿＿＿＿＿＿＿＿＿＿＿＿＿

＿＿＿＿＿＿＿＿＿＿＿＿＿＿＿＿＿＿＿＿＿＿＿＿＿＿＿＿＿

Postcode ＿＿＿＿＿＿＿＿ Signature ＿＿＿＿＿＿＿＿＿＿

MAILING PREFERENCE SERVICE

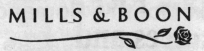

Next Month's Romances

Each month you can choose from a wide variety of romance with Mills & Boon. Below are the new titles to look out for next month, why not ask either Mills & Boon Reader Service or your Newsagent to reserve you a copy of the titles you want to buy – just tick the titles you would like and either post to Reader Service or take it to any Newsagent and ask them to order your books.

Please save me the following titles:	Please tick	√
DAWN SONG	Sara Craven	
FALLING IN LOVE	Charlotte Lamb	
MISTRESS OF DECEPTION	Miranda Lee	
POWERFUL STRANGER	Patricia Wilson	
SAVAGE DESTINY	Amanda Browning	
WEST OF BOHEMIA	Jessica Steele	
A HEARTLESS MARRIAGE	Helen Brooks	
ROSES IN THE NIGHT	Kay Gregory	
LADY BE MINE	Catherine Spencer	
SICILIAN SPRING	Sally Wentworth	
A SCANDALOUS AFFAIR	Stephanie Howard	
FLIGHT OF FANTASY	Valerie Parv	
RISK TO LOVE	Lynn Jacobs	
DARK DECEIVER	Alex Ryder	
SONG OF THE LORELEI	Lucy Gordon	
A TASTE OF HEAVEN	Carol Grace	

If you would like to order these books in addition to your regular subscription from Mills & Boon Reader Service please send £1.80 per title to: Mills & Boon Reader Service, Freepost, P.O. Box 236, Croydon, Surrey, CR9 9EL, quote your Subscriber No:................................... (If applicable) and complete the name and address details below. Alternatively, these books are available from many local Newsagents including W.H.Smith, J.Menzies, Martins and other paperback stockists from 3 December 1993.

Name:..

Address:..

....Post Code:.........................

To Retailer: If you would like to stock M&B books please contact your regular book/magazine wholesaler for details.

You may be mailed with offers from other reputable companies as a result of this application.
If you would rather not take advantage of these opportunities please tick box ☐